The Dream Maker

By

Lawrence Nielsen

A dream is a succession of images, ideas, emotions, and sensations that usually occur involuntarily in the mind during certain stages of sleep. Humans spend about two hours dreaming per night, and each dream lasts around 5 to 20 minutes.

BUT THEY ARE NOT WHAT YOU THINK THEY ARE!

Cover art and illustrations by Carolina Montoya Ramirez

First Addition

ISBN: 979-8-9866305-0-2

Available at: www.lulu.com

The Dream Maker

Contents

The Dream Maker

Lawrence Nielsen

Chapter 1
The Girls on the Train

It was a busy day for Daniel Anderson. Every day was busy; at least it had been for the last four months. That was when his boss came to him with what he said was a small project. Perhaps the boss's definition of small was different than everyone else's. The project exploded into the job of the century. Suddenly Dan was setting up a new enterprise system for the whole company, including their offices overseas.

But Dan didn't mind. In the seven years he had been with the company he had done many large projects. Never this large, but still large. Months ago, he threw himself at the project. He wasn't going to let it win. Some days, like this one, he felt like the project might have the upper hand, but to him it just meant he needed to push harder. That means long hours and little sleep.

He works for a large financial firm on LaSalle Street in Chicago. They are there to make money and they get their money's worth with Dan. The company hired him right out of college. It seems that they trusted him from his first day and he didn't want to let them down.

He knew the project was taking its toll on him. He was drinking a lot more coffee and he kept a stash of energy shots in his desk drawer. The project was taking its toll on his normal duties as well. He was a computer engineer and was supposed to be in charge of keeping the company computers running and safe from hackers. But those jobs had slipped to others, and he had to hope they were keeping up. But he told himself that pretty soon he could go back to his old job, and all would be good.

Although Dan works in downtown Chicago, he lives forty miles away, in the suburb of Elgin. The people of Elgin don't consider their town to be a suburb but, Chicago grows and engulfs like lava flowing from a volcano and surrounds little towns so that there is no way to distinguish them from a suburb.

Dan takes the train to and from work every day. The Metra is a full-size train. Not the smaller cars you would find in public transportation. It is quiet and comfortable. He actually looks forward to being in the relative quiet of the train. There was a time when Dan would catch the 3:30 train every day after work and be walking to his car in Elgin by 5:00. But not these days. He tries his best to catch the 8:40 train. If he misses it, the last train for the night is at 10:40. That would get him home after midnight, so he would barely have time for a nap before having to turn around and come right back to work, but it had happened several times lately.

Dan left work a little after 8:00 PM. He had plenty of time to make the ten-minute walk to Union Station. The news always talked about how dangerous it was in the city, but he had never had a problem and really, walking was faster than trying to take a bus or an Uber. In fact, on many days, he felt like the walk cleared his brain and he wished he could walk farther.

He got to the train. The doors were already open, so he boarded and looked for a seat. Most of the seats were benches that faced forward or back depending on which way the train was going. There were a few that sat sideways, and Dan liked those because they allowed him to stretch out his legs. He found a side bench and sat down. The car wasn't full, but Dan was a little surprised at the number of people onboard. Maybe they all had hot projects at work too.

The train quietly started rolling. Nine minutes later it made its first stop at Western Avenue. Stop and start, people on and off. That was the way home. When the train makes its sixteenth stop it would be Dan's turn to get off. Dan was tired, but he still pulled out his phone to review a service contract that they would be talking in the morning. He quickly realized that he couldn't concentrate, so he put the phone back in his pocket.

A second later the train was silent. The noise of the train and the people stopped. Dan looked around. There were no people. The train car was empty. He looked to his right and saw that there was a pretty lady sitting next to him. She was well dressed and was wearing what looked like an expensive fur lined jacket. She slid across the bench until she was close to him. She moved until she was pressing against him. She started flirting with him. At first Dan ignored her, but she persisted. He thought that maybe she was a prostitute. With that thought, he looked at her and told her he wasn't interested. The lady seemed to get angry. She jumped to her feet, pulled open the train car door and jumped out while the train was moving. Dan was stunned. He looked farther down the car and saw a young lady, standing alone, just shaking her head. Suddenly, the train noise started again, and the people reappeared. It was a dream.

It was a dream, but it seemed so real. Dan kept playing it in his head over and over. The train pulled into Elgin, and he went to his car. He couldn't stop thinking about it on the short drive home.

He lives with his mother in a small house. He knows that living with your mother isn't the best thing for getting dates. Girls just don't understand. But his work pretty much kept him out of the dating scene and at least for now living with his mother was the best thing for both of them. Even so, he wasn't about to tell his mother about the imaginary pretty woman on the train. It was a short evening.

The next day, as he took the train back into the city, the dream hadn't disappeared from his mind. But once he was at work, everything but work disappeared. As usual the day was an endless string of meetings and phone calls. Usually, by 5:00 PM most people have gone home, and Dan could get some quiet time to work. But today when the quiet time came, the dream returned. He decided that he didn't want another train dream, so it might be better to leave early while he was still awake. He left at 6:00 to catch the 6:40 train.

The train was much more crowded than the night before. Dan couldn't get his side bench, so he climbed to the upper level and took a seat. The seats on the second level were one deep so he figured that dream lady couldn't sit next to him. The train started to move, making its usual stops, Mont Clare, Elmwood Park, River Grove, silence. The people were gone.

It took a second for Dan to realize that now there was a pretty lady sitting on his lap. It was a different lady than the night before. She didn't seem to weigh anything. She was wearing a tight, bright blue silk dress. She put her arms around his neck, and he could feel her breath on his face. He asked her what she wanted, and she replied, "You". Dan told her that she didn't want him as he moved her off his lap as gently as he could.

She persisted, "We can have fun together. Let's go. The night is young."

Dan didn't know what to think. He blurted out, "I don't know who you are, or what you want, but you've got the wrong guy."

She started to cry with loud waling shrieks. She opened the window of the moving train and jumped out. That was strange too because the windows on Metra trains don't open. Dan looked down the passenger car. There was the same young lady as the night before. She had her head bowed and her face in her hands as she shook her head. The sounds and the people returned. It was another strange dream.

At work the next day Dan couldn't concentrate. He skipped several meetings and had trouble paying attention to the ones he did attend. He kept going over the dreams in his head. It just didn't make sense. Two dreams in two days that were almost the same, but different. They didn't even happen while he was in bed. In fact, just the idea that he could remember them didn't make sense. It wasn't unusual for him to remember a piece of a dream here or there, but never the whole scene and never twice in a row. Plus, they seemed so real. It all just didn't make sense.

He thought about his reactions in the dream. Twice he had a stunningly beautiful lady chasing after him and he did nothing. He reasoned that he probably would have done the same thing in real life, but this was a dream. Couldn't he be someone else in a dream? Maybe some handsome TV character? Maybe James Bond? No, he thought; he was Daniel Andersen and no one else, even in a dream.

He couldn't concentrate on work, so he sat at his desk, pulled out his phone to search for the meaning of dreams. He got fifteen million hits. Obviously, he wasn't the first person to wonder about dreams. He wondered if all those sites meant that that many people were having the kinds of dreams he was having.

He clicked on the word "train" and the screen read, "Your future is 'on track'. As trains follow a fixed route, this dream may suggest that you are being helped with your journey through life."

That wasn't very helpful. He tried again by clicking on the word, "Woman". The website said, "A woman may represent the other half of your personality- the side of you that is intuitive, sensitive, and nurturing. She may appear in a helpful or fearful guise depending upon the degree of acceptance you have for the irrational part of your soul."

Nothing he found on the web helped at all. Finally, Dan gave up and told his boss that he didn't feel right and left work in the early afternoon. He didn't want to. It was Thursday and the work was piling up. But at the same time, he wished he hadn't come to work today at all. He wished he didn't have to take that train home. After all, it happened both times on the train. It must have something to do with the train. He started his walk to the station but stopped at the Dunkin' Donuts on Jackson Blvd. to buy two large coffees. He drank one while he walked and saved the other for the train.

It was much less crowded on the train than the last two days. It was too early for the commuter crowd. But even though there were lots of open seats Dan stood at the end of the car. The train started to move, and he nervously sipped his coffee. By the sixth stop he ran out of coffee. Now he started walking the car, back and forth, and back and forth. He was worried that someone might report him as a suspicious character, but he was more worried that he would fall asleep.

Finally, the train pulled into Elgin. He did it. He made the whole journey without falling asleep. He got off the train and realized that he had another price to pay. Too much coffee. He needed a bathroom as soon as possible.

Dan was home so early he didn't know what to do with himself. His mother came home after him and was surprised to find him there. He just explained that he wasn't feeling good at work, so he left early, but a couple cups of coffee and relaxing on the train took care of it. Then he had a thought, that being home early might be just what the doctor ordered, so he grabbed a book that he had been meaning to read for the last few months, found a quiet place and just relaxed. The stress of work had been getting to him. It was probably what was causing the dreams. Spending an evening relaxing was just what he needed.

The next day Dan was back at work and feeling better. The dreams were still on his mind, but he wasn't as obsessed by them. Even so, he didn't want to take a late train. It was Friday, he skipped his solitary late day work time and left when everyone else left. But he still bought a cup of coffee on the way, just in case. He thought how yesterday staying awake was hard, but today he was rested and had his coffee. It should be easy.

The train was crowded again. It was rush hour. He intended to stand anyway, but with the car so crowded he didn't look out of place. He finished his coffee and stood holding the overhead hand bar and looking out the window. Since he was standing, all he could see out the window was the ground streaking by. It was mesmerizing. The train stopped and he had to move to let people out, then right back to watching the ground go by.

He looked up and the car was empty. Empty except for another pretty woman. This time she was scantily dressed. Dan couldn't tell exactly what she was wearing. It could have been a bikini or underwear or maybe a harem outfit. She was in the aisle dancing a seductive dance and calling for him to come to her with her hand motions. Dan stiffened. He thought that if he said something, she would just jump off the train. He didn't know what to do.

It seemed like an eternity went by. As she danced, she moved toward him. As she got close, Dan blurted out, "Go away!" in fear. A look of amazement came on her face and instead of jumping from the train she disappeared in a puff of red smoke. Through the smoke Dan could see that same young lady. She stood still in the middle of the aisle staring at him with a shocked look on her face. He put his hands up and yelled, "Wait, wait! Who are you? What is going on here?"

The lady froze as if she didn't know what to do. She looked like a child that had just been caught by her mother being naughty. It looked like she was trying to speak, but no words were coming out.

Dan tried again, "Don't let this end! I need to know what this is about."

The lady's voice stammered, "I'm, I'm sorry." Then after a pause. "I owe you an answer."

Dan stood silent giving full eye contact, hoping that it would keep her from disappearing.

"I have to go now," she said. "I have an assignment. But I promise I will answer your question. I will!"

Suddenly the train was crowded and noisy again. People were bumping into him as they exited the train. Dan wondered what he looked like when he was standing on a train dreaming. Did he have a blank stare or was he acting out what was happening. It didn't matter. He looked out and realized that he had dreamt right through his stop. The end of the line wasn't far from the Elgin Depot, but it still meant that he would have to catch an Uber to get back to his car.

As he headed home the words echoed in his head, 'I will answer your question. I will!' Great. What does that mean? He felt better that there was some resolution, but not a lot better. She promised him an explanation. He didn't know what that meant, but he guessed that it meant that this wasn't over and that she would be appearing in his dreams again.

Dan had dinner with his mother. They talked about work and things past, but Dan avoided any talk of the dreams or what seemed to be happening to him all week. He still hadn't dismissed the idea that he was having hallucinations and that there was something seriously wrong. It was a scary thought, and at best something not to dwell on.

* * *

For the last two months Dan had gone to work every Saturday, but this weekend he didn't want to be near the train. Besides, he thought, sleeping a little later would be good for him. He went to bed still thinking about the scene on the train.

There is no way to know how long he was asleep, but it seemed like the next instant he was standing on the deck of a ship. It was a cruise ship. There were no people and no sounds. He looked for the name of the ship, but it wasn't written anywhere. It was nice but at the same time it wasn't quite right. He was in the bow and as he looked toward the stern the scene seemed to lose definition like looking at a picture. The water wasn't right. It was blue, but there was no movement as if it were a painted floor.

Dan leaned on the rail staring into what should be the ocean. He heard a voice in back of him say, "It's beautiful here isn't it". It was the young lady from the train. She stood ten feet in back of him. He turned and was able to pay attention to her appearance for the first time. She was medium height with shoulder length hair. She was about Dan's age, late twenty's maybe early thirties. She was pretty; actually, the word cute might fit better. She didn't have the look of the fashion models that he had seen in the dreams, but she was attractive.

All Dan could blurt out was, "It's you."

She continued, "It's not going to sink this time, I promise."

Dan had a look of confusion.

"Most of the time it sinks. But the Technicians are off working on another dream, so it won't sink now."

Dan didn't understand but decided to let it go. He thought that if he could just understand what was happening, he could put an end to it. He said, "You said you would explain."

"I am so sorry. I really thought I was doing something good for you," she said. "I thought that a man like you would be flattered by a woman being attracted to him. I never thought you would be intimidated or afraid. I actually thought I was doing good. I am sorry."

Dan didn't like hearing the words intimidated and afraid. He didn't think that that was the case. It wasn't the women, it was the experience, well, that's what he told himself. Anyway, he decided not to argue the point. He calmed down and then said, "So you have the power to control my dreams?"

"It is more complicated than that," She replied. "Dreams are not what you think they are. There is a whole world that you know nothing about. You can't know. It's hidden."

Dan didn't know what to think.

"This ship," she waved her arm as if she were unveiling the cruise liner. "It is in many dreams. Some of the details change, but it is the same ship. Did you know that many people are afraid of being on a ship that is sinking? They are afraid even though it has never happened to them. Some of them have never been on a ship at all. They don't know what it's like. But they are afraid of it. In their dreams they experience it, and in their dreams, it is this ship."

"No," Dan said. "Dreams are in the mind. There is no sinking ship. Those people just imagine it."

"That is what the experts think, but they have never seen this ship. They have never seen it like you are seeing it, and they have never met me, or anyone like me."

Dan didn't believe it. At the same time, he had experienced the dreams and he was standing on a ship that looked like it could be a movie prop. But he could be imagining the ship. He could be imagining the girl. He could be crazy and imagining everything. How could he know?

Then he started to wonder, if he were crazy would he be able to question the whole thing? No, he would just believe it. But it can't be real. Then he asked himself what would it hurt to play along? If he is crazy playing along would be natural. If he isn't crazy, then there is something really strange going on and it might be worth investigating. He kept debating with himself. Is it possible to experience these things and not be crazy?

The girl interrupted his thoughts, "I know it is hard to believe. There are no books. No reports. No genius investigators figuring out the details and posting them on the web so they can go viral among the conspiracy believers. It is carefully hidden. But let me show you a little more."

She took Dan's hand. Her hand was warm and felt like a normal human hand. She led him through a door in the ship. It wasn't exactly a door. It looked like a wall until she stepped toward it, then it opened as if it appeared out of nowhere.

They took one step through the door and Dan found himself in a dark hall. It was wide with a high ceiling. The walls were dark grey, close to black. There were lights every so often, but they left dark areas in between. High above there were trays with cables and ducts running along the way. The place reminded him of service tunnels that ran under the buildings in the city. In many places there are tunnels that allow workers and their materials to get from one place to another without the public ever seeing them.

The girl escorted him down the hall. It was very long. It went on as far as Dan could see in either direction. They weren't alone there were people traveling back and forth. Some were carrying objects. Sometimes there were two or three carrying larger items.

Every few yards there were large double doors. They were way too big for people. Dan wondered if this was a land of giants. Some of the doors were open. He tried to look in but could only get a glimpse as the girl kept him moving. There were all kinds of workshops. Some had benches with people working on small projects. Some looked like tailor shops with all kinds of clothes being made and put on racks. He looked in one and all he could see was the bottom of scaffolding as if something very large was under construction.

Some of the rooms were just storage. Dan couldn't stop to look at the things being stored, but he could see that there were all kinds of items. They were neatly stacked so they could be retrieved, but every room was full. The items he could make out looked like they were storing a combination of a thrift shop, a carnival, and a museum.

As they walked there were intersections with more tunnels going off to the left or the right. They were dark and Dan couldn't see what was down those halls.

They walked down one of the halls. The girl told Dan to be very quiet. They turned a corner and Dan found himself in a business conference room. There were people sitting around a table discussing something. At the head of the table was a man in a sharp business suit. The girl whispered in Dan's ear, "It is his dream. He is the one who is dreaming. Everyone else are Players."

Dan didn't understand but couldn't ask without talking. The girl quietly led Dan to a place in back of the man. The girl whispered, "Usually I am one of the Players, but for this dream they let me help the Technicians. That way it is easier to show you how it works."

The discussion in the meeting continued. Dan couldn't understand what they were talking about. The girl picked up a rope from the floor. She handed it to Dan, and said, "Take the rope. When I tell you, yank on it as hard as you can."

Dan took the rope, feeling as confused as ever. After a couple minutes the girl gave him a signal and he pulled on the rope. The rope was attached to the dreamer's suit and with one pull the suit came off and the man was sitting in the meeting naked. Dan looked on in amazement. At first the man continued as if nothing had changed. Then he suddenly seemed to realize he was naked. He pondered what to do. He couldn't get up and leave. No one had noticed. He took a pile of papers and put them in his lap. He was confused and nervous. This went on for several minutes. After a time, a ghostly looking figure snuck up to him, whispered something in his ear and he disappeared.

Dan tried to stay quiet, but he couldn't. He whispered, "Where did he go?"

The girl answered in a normal voice, "His dream ended. He is back in his bed. He may be asleep, or he may be awake relieved it was just a dream. We need to move out of the way. The Technicians have to move the furniture."

They stepped off to the side and Dan watched as a group of people came and executed a carefully choreographed change of the room. They didn't just move the furniture, they changed everything. Within minutes it was a different place. Now it was a church with pews, a pulpit and stained-glass windows.

The Players quickly took their seats in the pew, and one went up to the pulpit to play the part of the preacher. Dan and the girl stood in the back. The preacher started to lead the Players in a song. Dan didn't recognize the music. As he watched he noticed a lady in one of the middle pews. She was holding a hymn book and was singing loudly. It was easy to see that she wasn't a Player. She had to be the dreamer.

The girl handed Dan a rope and said, "We'll let her finish a couple of songs first."

The singing went on. In the middle of a song the girl poked Dan's arm to tell him to pull. He did and the lady's dress quietly came off. At first, she kept singing. Dan watched as her singing became muffled. She looked around. No one seemed to notice, but she knew. She couldn't understand how she could have come to church and forgotten to put on her clothes. She slid to the end of the pew and looked around to see if the coast was clear for her to make a break for it. She got up to run for the exit. One of the Players whispered in her ear, and she disappeared.

A Technician took the rope from Dan's hand and removed the dress.

Dan asked the girl, "Do we need to get out of the way again?"

She answered, "No, We're going to use the same set. But it's a little different. This time it is more complicated, so I'll handle the rope. You sit in the pew. It is important that you don't react. No matter what you see, pretend that everything is normal."

Dan sat in the back pew. Just like last time the Players sat in the pews. The preacher started preaching a sermon. Dan looked around the room. He was no expert, but to him everyone looked like Players. He couldn't find the dreamer. The preaching had its characteristic highs and lows. A strong voice for emphasis and quieter words to draw people in.

Since he couldn't find the dreamer, he looked up at the pulpit. The girl was up there in back of the preacher holding a rope. The preacher was the dreamer. The girl pulled the rope. The preacher was standing behind the pulpit without any clothes.

At first the sermon continued. Dan fought to keep a straight face. The preacher's voice became quiet, then stopped all together. All the Players acted as if they hadn't noticed, but the preacher was visibly embarrassed. He looked around the pulpit for any help. Evidently, he couldn't see the girl. But there was a door on either side of the pulpit behind him. The preacher hesitated, then decided to make a break for it. He ran to the door to make his escape, but when he got there, it was locked. He pushed on it, and pounded on the door, but it wouldn't open. At that moment, a Player came up, whispered in his ear and he disappeared.

The girl walked back to where Dan was sitting. "The next dreamer will be here in a minute, but I am afraid you are going to have to go. I have another assignment in another place and there isn't time to take you with. We'll meet again soon"

Dan woke up. He was in his bed. He looked at the clock; it was 3:00 AM. Maybe the whole thing was a dream. If it was, it wasn't like a normal dream. Just like the dreams on the train, he could remember all of it and it wasn't fading from his memory.

Sleep was impossible now. At first, he lay there hoping to drift off but the dreams, or whatever they were, kept playing in his head. He got up, grabbed his phone, and started doing more searches on Dreams. But just like before, he thought that everything he found was dumb. The writers on those websites might have done some surveys of what the most common dreams are, but the reasons for the dreams were ridiculous. They didn't know. They were just making stuff up.

Dan spent the day around the house. His mother noticed that he was acting different, but he wasn't about to tell anyone what he had experienced. He thought that even his own mother would have him committed.

Later in the afternoon he had enough of sitting around and went for a long walk. He always found that walking cleared his head and helped him to think. He came to a park and found a bench where he could sit and watch children playing under the watchful eyes of their mothers. There were people walking their dogs and an occasional jogger.

Dan watched the people. He thought about how every one of them had dreams every night. The idea that all those dreams were made by a troupe of Players acting out scenes was absurd. The size of the operation would be enormous. There are over seven billion people in the world, and it looked like it took more than one Player to make a dream. Of course, people don't dream all night so it would take less… No, it is still absurd.

Then he started to think about some of the dreams from the past that he remembered. Some of them were from common parts of his life. But some, some of them were places he had never seen before, and many had people he didn't know. Was his brain creative enough to make up a face in detail? Could his resting brain create images of new places? He can't draw a picture. He can't even decorate a cake, but his brain can produce a whole movie. He decided that the answer was no. His brain could do it and that's that, and all the brains of all the people in the park could do it too. They had to be able to do it. It happened every night.

Dan went home and moped around the house. He wished he could just go to sleep like a normal person and forget about his problems. But he didn't think he was a normal person and he dreaded going to sleep. Finally, he gave up. He knew what was going to happen, but he was tired of fighting it. It wasn't particularly late when he crawled into bed.

Chapter 2
Not What You Think

Dan fell asleep instantly. There is no way to know if he was asleep for hours or if it was the next instant, but he found himself in that same long service tunnel with the workshops, tailor shops, and storage rooms on both sides. The lady was directly in front of him with a smile on her face as if she were happy to see him.

"Come on," she said. "We have a real easy one to do right now."

She grabbed his hand like a mother leading a child and they started down the hall. "We have an assignment, so we need to get going."

"Where are we going?" Dan inquired.

"We have an assignment. Don't worry, it's easy. We'll probably just be extras in the background and..." she stopped with a flash of distraction. "We're a little early. I want to show you something while we are here. It's really fun."

She led Dan a little way down a side hall. It was dark, but there was a small round window. She pointed and told Dan to look in there. Dan looked. It was a round room. It was too tall and deep for him to see the ceiling or the floor. The walls were light blue but had white areas that looked like clouds. As Dan looked he saw a lady floating in midair. It was strange. She was just hanging there in horizontal position. Dan could see her face. She looked terrified.

"What am I looking at?" Dan asked.

"She's falling. That's the falling room"

"The what?"

The girl smiled, "The lady is dreaming that she is falling. Lots of people dream they are falling. It is a real easy dream for us. It doesn't take any Players or any acting. We just put the dreamers in the falling room and leave them alone. They fall and fall. Sometimes the Technicians will put pictures on the walls or floor, but most of the time they just fall. I suppose it might scare some people, but it shouldn't. They should realize that falling is fun."

"I don't think most people will figure out that it is fun," Dan said. "She will probably wake up with cold sweats." He paused for a moment. "Although, I guess if I knew that it was a falling room, it might be fun to try."

"We have to go." the girl said. "We'll be late for our assignment."

As they walked, Dan started thinking about how this time he actually had some conversation with the girl. She wasn't as scary now as he had imagined. He decided to try to keep it going. See what he could learn.

"What is your name," he asked.

"What?" she said

"You never told me your name. You know my name. You seem to know a lot about me, but I don't even know your name."

"My name is Abbi," the girl said. "Dream Players have names you wouldn't be able to pronounce, so you can call me Abbi."

Dan wanted to keep the conversation going, but he didn't know what to say. He wasn't very good at making conversation and he was even worse at doing it with a woman. He was in a dream. He couldn't exactly talk about the weather. But they were walking together now, so now was the time to talk.

"How long have you been a Dream Player?" He asked, but as soon as the words came out of his mouth his next thought was, 'What a stupid question. She's probably some spirit creature that has always existed, or maybe she really is part of my dream in which case there wouldn't be an answer.'

Abbi opened her mouth as if she was going to answer, but no words came out. She thought for a second with no result. It was strange. She felt like she knew the answer but couldn't remember it. But that can't be right. Rather than standing there being embarrassed she nodded that they have to keep moving.

Dan tried again, "You seem to like being in people's dreams"

Now Abbi was more animated. She answered, "I do. It is so interesting seeing how people react. Even though they are asleep I am helping them cope with the time they are awake. Plus, I like working with the other Dream Players and the Dream Maker has been very good to me."

"The Dream Maker?" Dan asked.

"Yes," Abbi answered. "We all work for him. He is the source of all dreams. He tells us what the dream will be and helps us get them done. Not for every dream, you understand. Sometimes he lets certain trusted Players improvise dreams. Those are the Dream Masters. They are in charge of making the dreams work. There are some Players that rebel against the Masters and go off on their own. They write their own dreams without following a Dream Master, but those are very bad Players."

"Tell me more about the Dream Maker," Dan said.

"I will, but I can't right now. It is time to start the next dream," Abbi said.

They turned a corner and walked through an invisible door. With that Dan found himself in a large round room. It was large, but not overly so. It looked like a small ballroom with fine Victorian wood paneling all around. There were no windows, but some of the panels were shiny like they were made of polished gold. There was what looked like one set of double doors on the other end of the room. The doors didn't look Victorian at all. They were flat and plain.

They walked toward a small group of people. They were other Dream Players. They greeted Abbi, but ignored Dan. Abbi left Dan and went to one of the Players. Dan hardly noticed. He was busy looking at the odd room. A few moments later Abbi returned with a bundle in her arms.

"Put this on," she said, as she handed the bundle to Dan.

Dan unfurled the bundle. It was a one-piece jump suit. It looked like the coveralls a mechanic might wear. Dan assumed that he was to put the suit on over his clothes. Thinking that made him think about the fact that he was wearing slacks and a polo shirt. That seemed odd. If he were dreaming, shouldn't he be wearing the pajama bottoms and tee shirt he wore to bed? Abbi made a motion trying to get him to hurry up, so he put the thoughts of his clothes aside and put on the coveralls.

Abbi gave a brief explanation. "The room we are in is an elevator. We are just extras. All we do is stand together and look at the dreamer. Don't say anything. He will be aware that there are people watching him. That's why we are here."

One of the Players motioned with her arm to come to the side of the room. Everyone gathered together. When Dan got there, he noticed that he was standing by one of the shiny panels. He looked at himself, but instead of seeing mechanics coveralls, he was wearing business casual clothes. He saw slacks, a button-down shirt, and a tie. He had the thought that he looked pretty good, but then also had the thought that this is what the dreamer is going to see.

The doors opened. They slid open from the middle. They were elevator doors. A man walked in. It was obvious that he was the dreamer. He glanced at the people watching him and turned to a control panel next to the door. He pressed a button. Nothing happened. He pressed another. Nothing.

He glanced at the people. He obviously felt some pressure because people were watching. He kept pressing buttons with no result.

After some time, one of the Players, who was dressed in a full business suit walked up and pressed a button. With that the elevator took off like a rocket. Although there were no windows, Dan felt his whole body gain weight as the elevator accelerated. The Player in the suit was gone, and the dreamer was desperately trying to stop the elevator by pushing every button. He looked at the crowd, still feeling the pressure from being watched. Finally, he saw a big red button. Dan was thinking that that button wasn't there a second ago. The dreamer pressed the button, the elevator stopped, with a sudden jerk, and the doors opened. He went out and the doors closed behind him.

Dan heard one of the Players say, "Good job, everyone. You can all go to your next assignment."

Dan turned to Abbi, "Is his dream over?"

"No. There is a complex set of stairs out there that don't really go anywhere and are up very high. He is out there trying to figure out how to get through them."

"What now?" Dan asked.

"I have another assignment in a few minutes, but you can't come with for this one. You need to go back to bed." She answered.

"Wait, wait," Dan tried to get words in as quickly as he could. "Please. Please leave me alone on the train..."

Dan woke up in his own bed. It was 4:30 AM. He was wearing the pajama bottoms and tee shirt he went to bed in. He sat up. Was it a dream? He didn't know. A few minutes later he fell back asleep and stayed that way until his alarm went off at 6:00.

* * *

It was Monday and Dan started his day with his usual routine. Wash up, get dressed, get a little breakfast while watching local news on TV, then run for the train. The train ride to Chicago was normal, as was his walk to the office. Everything seemed normal, but his life wasn't normal. The dreams followed him everywhere he went.

He called in to the daily 9:00 telecon. Fortunately, there were no computer outages over the weekend, so he didn't have to solve any emergencies. After the meeting he went to the company web site. He searched for EAP, the Employee Assistance Program. He never thought he would need such a thing. For years he would hear his management mention it in staff meetings just in case anyone was having trouble dealing with the pressures of work or home. Every time he heard it a little joke would play in the back of his head. He would never say it out loud, but when he heard it in the meeting, the next thought in his head was, 'You'd have to be crazy to use a thing like that.'

Dan wrote the number on a post-it note, and put it in his pocket. His next thought was, 'Now what?' He couldn't call from his office. Someone would hear. The bathroom wouldn't be any better. He checked the conference room schedule from his computer, but they were booked all day. He thought of maybe a restaurant or a coffee shop. Would it matter if strangers overheard him? Then he remembered a small park, actually more of a small greens space, on the corner of Jackson and Wacker. He walked by it every day on his way to the train. It was always empty. People in the city are too busy to sit and watch plants. It was less than two blocks away. He finished up some emails and headed out for the park.

The park was small, but it did have places to sit. The nice thing was that, like always, everyone just walked by in a hurry to go wherever they go and didn't take the time to stop. The park was empty. Dan pulled out his cellphone and the slip of paper and sat down. He stopped for a minute trying to decide if he really wanted to call. Then he started thinking of the dreams and dialed the number.

He heard a voice, "Protectcare employee and family resources, this is Christina how may I help you today?

"I," Dan hesitated, "I need some help."

"Thank you for calling." Christina said. "I'm going to gather some information and see how we can help."

She took his name, company, and a few basic details, then asked, "Tell me Dan, what brings you to call Protectcare today?"

"I've been having these dreams. They're different than anything I've ever experienced. I think I might be going crazy."

"I'm sorry to hear that you are having these problems, Dan," Christina said. "You called the right place. I am a licensed counselor. Would you like to talk this through right now?

Dan was uncomfortable enough. He didn't want to tell everything to a voice on the phone, but he didn't want to be rude either. He replied, "You sound like a nice person, but I don't think I want to talk about this on the phone. Besides, it could take a long time to explain."

Christina continued, "Before we go any further, I want to make sure you are all right. I can tell you are going through a hard time, and I want to make sure you aren't thinking of doing anything to hurt yourself."

Dan knew what she was asking and he wanted to reassure her. "I'm not thinking of killing myself. I wouldn't do that. Just a little while ago one of our senior managers at work committed suicide. I don't think he had any family, but I saw what it did to everyone who worked with him. Funny, he must have lived out in my direction because I would see him on the train sometimes. He learned my name and always took the time to greet me."

"I'm sorry to hear that. Everyone matters," Christina said. "OK. We can set you up with counseling sessions, and when you go to your counseling sessions you can talk through everything that is going on. Whatever it takes to help you work through the problem."

"Sounds good," Dan replied.

"OK. I have authorized you for counseling sessions. You can go ahead and call the counselor who I have set you up with for an appointment, or if you prefer, I can call with you on the phone right now."

"Let's set it up now," Dan said. He knew that if the appointment wasn't made right now, he would chicken out.

"Great," Christina said. "I've looked in our files and I think the best kind of help for you would be with a Cognitive Psychologist. I have located one in Cicero. She is very good. I see that she has worked with other people from your company in the past. Now if you don't mind, I would like to put you on hold while I warm transfer the call to her office."

"OK," Dan said.

A few minutes later Christina was back. "Dan, are you there?"

He replied.

"I have the office of Dr. Margret Keller on the line. You can talk to them and set up your appointment. If there is anything else we can do for you, please keep in mind that our 800 number is available around the clock."

There was a click on the phone and a different voice started to speak, "Hello Mr. Andersen. This is Dr. Keller's office. We have an opening the day after tomorrow at 3:30. Would you be available at that time?"

Dan thought about how that was two more nights of dreams to go through. Then he thought how one session wasn't going to make the dream go away anyway so he told the new voice to set up the appointment.

"Alright Mr. Andersen, we have the appointment set," the new voice said. "We are located on Cermak Road in Cicero. I will email you the details, including some paperwork you need to fill out before you arrive. We look forward to meeting you. Have a nice day."

The phone went silent. Dan sat and stared for a few minutes. He needed to get back to work, but then he decided he needed to decompress first. There was a Shake Shack across the street, so he walked over. He just wanted a simple chocolate shake, but everything had a fancy name, and it was hard to tell what anything was. He ended up ordering something called a Chocolate Pie Shake. It was close enough. He found a quiet corner, sat and, ate his shake. Soon he felt better and had no problem finishing his workday and even working a little late. He took the train home. There were no dreams on the train. He wondered if Abbi heard him, if it was the power of suggestion in his mind, or just dumb luck.

He and his mother had dinner together. He still didn't want to tell her anything. On the other hand, if she learned that he was going to a, what was it called? A Cognitive Psychologist. She would be a little upset. But the timing wasn't right, so he made sure they talked about other things.

He watched the 10:00 news on TV and went to bed. He was less fearful than before. Maybe there is less to fear when you know what is about to happen. He drifted off. The next thing he knew he was sitting on a bench on a dock. The dock was jutting out into a beautiful small lake. The lake was surrounded with dense forest. On one side there were cattails that gave the lake a pleasant character. Dan sat and stared at the scene. It was amazingly peaceful.

After a few minutes he heard a voice, "You're not crazy." It was Abbi.

"You've been watching me," Dan said.

"No," she replied. "I can't do that, but let's just say I got a report."

Dan turned to Abbi. He noticed that she was wearing the same clothes as every other time he had met her. He thought that was odd. He thought he should have a more creative imagination than that, so he should imagine her in different clothes. Well, maybe not. Dan spent enough time thinking about it that there was a pause in their conversation.

"You are not crazy," Abbi repeated, as she sat down next to him.

Dan faced the lake not really talking to Abbi. "Hmm, what does it mean when you have an imaginary friend tell you that you are not crazy?"

Abbi got a satisfied look on her face as if she had been given a great compliment.

"I'm glad you consider me your friend, but I am not imaginary!" Abbi replied. "You don't understand. Dreams are not what you have always been told they were. A lot of very smart people have studied and dissected dreams. They have their theories about what they are. They believe they know what they mean. They are all wrong. It is like they only looked at a play from the audience side and didn't even know it was a play. If they had ever gone backstage, they would have very different ideas."

Dan shook his head. "You tell me I'm backstage, but how do I know I'm not watching a play about being backstage?"

"I don't have an answer for that." Abbi replied. "How do you know your life with your computer job and your mother isn't a dream?"

"I refuse to believe I live in The Matrix," Dan replied.

"The what?" Abbi asked.

"Never mind. It would be too hard to explain." Dan tried to change the subject. "This is an amazingly beautiful place. It is so peaceful. After spending so much time in the city it does feel good."

"I was hoping you would like it," Abbi said. "It is one of my favorites. Especially now when there are no Technicians around to make things go wrong."

"What could go wrong with a place like this?" Dan asked.

"The dream Techs have all kinds of things rigged here, but don't worry, they aren't around to control them."

"What do you mean?" Dan asked.

"Well, the water has piranhas, a shark, and a sea monster in it. The reeds have a place for natives to stand and shoot arrows or blowgun darts. There are attacking condors in the trees. Oh, and the boards on the dock are rigged to suddenly be loose so no matter how hard you run you don't get anywhere. There might be more, but those are the ones I've seen used."

Dan had a puzzled look on his face. "Why do all of you spend all your time torturing people?"

"We don't torture people," Abbi replied. "We help people."

Dan started out in almost a mocking tone, "Let's see. You put a person in an idyllic setting. A place so beautiful that nothing could possibly go wrong. Then suddenly they are being chased by a sea monster, shot at by natives, and are unable to do anything but run in place. Seems like a strange kind of help to me."

"I know this is new to you and you don't understand," Abbi said. "I'll try to explain it, or at least some of it. You see, dreams are necessary. Every human being has to dream to survive. Even your know-nothing experts will tell you that. What those experts don't know is why it is necessary. Even that is complicated because it is not the same for every person but let me tell you a few of them.

"For one, human beings need adventure. You know that is true just by looking at top selling movies and books. That need for adventure attracts people to mystery books or superhero movies. What they don't know is how much adventure they really need. It is a lot. All through history humans have had to live their day to day lives and as a result they fall short of the amount of adventure they need to survive. Some humans try to meet the need by doing extreme things, but they can't do extreme things all the time, so they come up short. Probably if they really tried, at some point they would make a mistake and have a very short life. Dreaming fulfills that need. Being chased by a bear or being stuck in a malfunctioning elevator fulfills the need for adventure without actual danger that could end their life.

"Another way we help humans is by helping them face their fears. Humans are funny creatures. They crave adventure, but at the same time they are fearful beings. A lot of times they don't even know everything they are afraid of. We give them a chance to experience their fear and if they realize that they came through them they can overcome them. But we don't give them all their fears. Having some fear is a good thing. It helps a person to be careful when they need to and to avoid things they should. So, we act out silly fears, so people only have to keep the fears that are good for them.

"Sometimes humans have problems they can't deal with in their conscious life. We act them out with them and help them deal with them. We can't solve their problems. In fact, many times humans ignore the experience and waste the opportunity. Have you ever heard someone say that they will sleep on it? Those are the people who accept our help.

"We also act out traumas humans had in the past. Something bad happened to them and we act it out so they can live it again. They don't like living it again. It is one of the hardest dreams that we make. But if they were left to deal with it on their own, and only when they are awake and have to deal with the rest of life, well, most humans couldn't do it.

"There is one more. You might find that this one is the hardest to swallow because of all your know nothing experts and your society that thinks they know everything. But sometimes the Dream Maker himself wants to tell you something. He has us craft his message into a special dream that he himself designed. We have changed the direction of the lives of humans, but sadly, too many times these days our messages are ignored and written off as being caused by too much pizza for dinner."

Dan didn't say anything. He still didn't really believe that what he was seeing was real, and now his illusion was telling him that his aberration was just the outer skin of the onion and that there were layers below him that no one could even suspect.

There was a bird call from the top of one of the trees. Dan asked, "Is the condor about to attack?"

"No," Abbi answered. "It is one of my Dream Player friends telling me that we have to go. We are scheduled for a dream in a few minutes."

They stood up and started down the short dock toward the shore. As they walked Dan looked at the planks below his feet to see if any were loose or if he could see anything that might make them into a conveyer, but he couldn't see anything. They looked like regular weathered boards that you would see on any dock.

They got to the end of the dock. There was a trail heading off into the woods. They took one step onto the trail and Dan found himself back in the service tunnel. It was busy with what Dan guessed were Technicians carrying props back and forth. There were characters dressed in all different costumes coming from or heading off to someone's dream. As they walked down the corridor Abbi pushed him to one side to allow a waddle of penguins to pass by.

Eventually they came to a door and Abbi ushered him in. Dan found himself in a classroom. It was a grade school style classroom with individual desks. Abbi gave him some coveralls and he put them on, but there was no mirror, so he didn't know what the dreamer thought he was wearing.

"Sit here," Abbi said. "There is a pencil and paper on the desk. We will all be taking a test. Follow what you see on the paper. For the first dream act like the test is easy for you. We will be off to the side. The dreamer will be sitting in the front row."

"First dream? Dan said. But Abbi was already seated in a desk that was too far away for her to answer.

Dan sat down. A moment later a man appeared in one of the front row desks. He was middle aged. Definitely not school age. Dan guessed that school experiences stay with people for the rest of their lives, so naturally they would appear in dreams years later.

The teacher stood in the front of the class. She explained that this was a timed test and that anyone who does not finish in the allotted time would automatically fail. She held up a stopwatch, clicked a button, and declared that the test had started.

Dan picked up his pencil and looked at the paper in front of him. It had instructions to start writing, so he did. A few seconds later the paper said to take a break and look thoughtful. Shortly after that the paper told Dan to look like he thought of the answer and go back to writing.

Dan followed the instructions, but he could also see that the dreamer was having problems. His pencil wouldn't write. He looked around realizing that no one else was having problems. He tried again, but now the pencil started sinking into the paper. He pulled it back, but the paper had turned into slime and stuck to the pencil. He tried to pick up the paper, but now the slime was sticking to his hands. He looked around again to see if anyone else had the problem or if anyone could help. Everyone else looked normal, having no problem taking the test. This went on for the longest time. At one point he tried to get up but found that he was stuck to his chair. He tried to call out to the teacher, but nothing came out of his mouth. One of the Players snuck up behind him and whispered something to him. He started to breathe heavily and seconds later disappeared.

Dan heard a voice, "Good job everyone. Relax for five minutes, until the next dreamer arrives."

Dan was sitting too far from Abbi to talk to her. He wanted to ask some questions, but it was going to have to wait. Soon the next dreamer appeared. This time it was a college age looking girl. Her hair was in a ponytail, and she wore a white track suit.

Again, the teacher explained about this being a timed test and the importance of finishing on time. Then she started the test.

Dan looked at his paper. It said to act like the test was very hard and as if he didn't know the answer. He did the best he could. He had never done any acting. Well, in grade school he helped put on a puppet show, but that wasn't going to help here.

The dreamer started taking the test. She wrote volumes, turned the page, and wrote some more. She wasn't having any problems at all. Occasionally she looked around the room to see how others were doing. Everyone's paper must have told them to act like the test was hard because no one was writing and many of the Players had a pained look on their face.

The teacher announced that there was thirty minutes left. One of the Players whispered to her. She confidently straightened her test papers, stood up and handed them to the teacher. She looked around the classroom with a look of triumph and disappeared.

Dan thought about how nothing bad had happened to her. Then he thought about people he remembered from school who were always confident in everything they did. He was always just a little jealous of them. Now he could see that they were just as confident in their dreams, and he envied them even more. He could never be that way. There was always a little voice in the back of his brain that told him that he should be better.

The Dream Master gave everyone a short break before the next dreamer arrived. It was another female. This one was much younger than the others. Possibly grade school age.

The teacher stood up and introduced the test. There was no mention of it being timed, but more than once the teacher told the students how important it was and that it had to be done exactly right.

Dan noticed that the student was younger, and the teacher explained the test more like a grade school teacher and not like it was a college test.

The test started and the girl started to write. Her pencil worked and nothing turned to slime. She wrote an answer, looked at it a second time and saw that what she had written had changed. Now it was the wrong answer. She erased it and tried again. It changed again. She frantically kept trying to get the right answer on the page, but it wouldn't stay. This kept happening.

She looked around the room. Everyone was following the instructions on their paper and acting like they were engrossed in taking the test.

The girl tried again, but she couldn't get the right answer to stick. She tried to raise her hand to get the teacher's attention, but it was as if her arm was suddenly too heavy to raise. Eventually a Player whispered to her, and she disappeared.

Dan lost count of the number of dreamer test takers he saw. They all sat in the same seat. Dan guessed that that was the seat that the Technicians had rigged. But each dream was just a little bit different. Dan was surprised at how interesting it was to watch the people react. He considered himself to be an engineer not a people person. Usually, he felt more at home with code on the screen of a computer in the back room than he did with people, but somehow this was different.

Another dreamer disappeared and Abbi looked over to Dan with an embarrassed look on her face. She said, "I'm sorry. I lost track of time. I didn't mean to keep you this long."

He woke up in his bed. It was 6:30. He had overslept by half an hour.

Chapter 3
Problems upon Problems

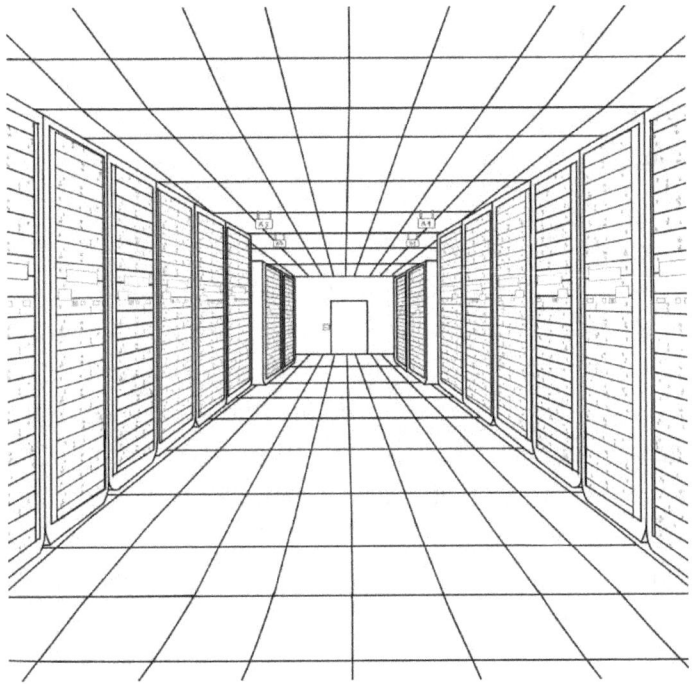

Dan rolled out of bed, but quickly gave up on making the 7:26 train. The 8:28 train was the best he was going to do, so he slowed down and went about his morning routine. After he was safely on the train, he sent a text to his boss to tell him that he was going to be in late. He felt angry at Abbi for making him late, but then realized that he was angry at an imaginary person. Nothing made sense.

Dan had to call in to the 9:00 telecon from the train. He didn't like that for several reasons. For one, there was no privacy. Most mornings he calls in and just listens, but if there are any questions about computer systems he would have to talk and everyone around him would hear. When he calls in from his desk, he has his computer open and if there are questions, he can look them up real-time. That makes him look good. On top of all that, if anyone needs anything immediately he would have to admit that he was late and not at work.

Dan dialed the number and put in the six-digit passcode. The meeting hadn't started, so all he heard was nauseating music playing the same handful of notes over and over until the meeting leader called in. Most days the meeting starts with one of the executives greeting everyone, saying that he hoped everyone had a good evening, then introducing the first agenda item. Not today. There was a clunk and the nauseating music stopped. Instead of the usual, "Good Morning," there was a frantic voice. "Computers are down all over the company! Dan Andersen, are you on the line?"

Dan cringed as he pressed the mute button on his phone and replied, "I'm here."

What followed was a panicked and not very helpful description of computers not responding and work not getting done.

Dan struggled to stay calm. He felt like the whole company was blaming him for something he didn't even know about. He took a deep breath and started to speak, pretending to be calm, "I had not heard of this until just now. Look, I was coming in a little later today, so I'm still on the train. I'm passing Franklin Park right now. Let me make some calls to get to the bottom of the problem. The train arrives at 9:45, so I can be on-site by 10:00. Let's schedule an 11:00 tag-up and I will have a solid status for you then."

Dan was surprised at how much the wild beasts had calmed down. Maybe they just felt less helpless.

Dan hung up from the telecon and started going down his contacts list looking for anyone who might be in the office or better yet the datacenter. It took three calls before someone picked up. "This is Dan Andersen. Is this Mike?" It was. "I'm glad I got a hold of you. Can you tell me what is happening with the computer systems? I've heard from management, but it wasn't very helpful. You can see the problem, so I think you can do better."

Mike explained what he had seen. Dan continued, "Mike, that means the servers are off-line. Not just one. They load share. They must all be off-line. Have you looked in the server room?"

"I don't work in the server room. I don't have access," he replied.

"Take down my number and call me from your cell so we can talk while you walk, then get down to the server room and tell me when you're there."

Mike called back and walked to the server room. Dan gave him the cypher-lock numbers to get in. This was no time to worry about security. Mike's voice came back, "It's hot as blazes in here. The computers are on. They have lights blinking, but not the usual fast blinking like comm signals."

Dan had Mike read the displays off some of the machines, then he told Mike, "The room lost cooling. The servers overheated and shut down. There should have been an alarm, but something went wrong. OK, I'll be there in half an hour. Right now, prop the door open, and see if you can find a fan to blow office air in there. Then call the building superintendent and see if he can fix the cooling. Thanks for your help, Mike, you're a lifesaver. See you in a few."

The train pulled in at 9:45. Dan thought of jogging to the office but thought better of it. He didn't want to look like a mess when he arrived. A brisk walk would have to do. When he got to the server room Mike was waiting for him along with the building superintendent and several IT staff people.

"Hi Mike," Dan said, then he looked at the other man and extending his hand to shake. "You must be the building superintendent. I'm Dan Andersen."

"Nice to meet you," The man said. "We've tracked down the problem. The motor on the A.C. compressor froze up and drew too much current. Instead of popping its own breaker it popped the main breaker. That took out everything on the subpanel including your alarms."

"Makes sense," Dan said. He looked at the server room door. There was a chair propping it open with a tiny office fan blowing air into it.

The Superintendent noticed Dan looking at it. "I sent one of my guys to get a real fan. I also called a rental company to see about getting a portable cooling unit. They have one and it will be here around noon. We'll have to get an HVAC man in here to fix the regular unit. That could take as much as a week."

"That's great. Thanks. Here is my number. If you need anything or if anything else goes wrong give me a call." Then Dan turned to the people standing there and said, "We're going to meet in the conference room in 10 minutes. We need to put together a reactivation plan ASAP."

The crowd dispersed and Dan stepped into the server room. It was very hot and had an oppressive dry feeling. He went back to his desk, grabbed his laptop and headed for the conference room. The meeting went well. Dan was proud of the expertise he saw in the people there. They finished just in time for Dan's meeting with management.

The meeting with management was tense, but not as frantic as the call earlier that morning. Dan laid out their recovery plan. They would have to bring up one server at a time and run diagnostics on each before allowing it to go back into operation. They had a list of priorities that would allow the company to restart operations as soon as possible.

The Dream Maker

The presentation on restarting the servers went well and there were no questions. But then followed several long soliloquies about how this needs to be fixed so that it can never happen again. Dan had to tell himself to be patient. Obviously, everyone knows that this has to be fixed so it won't happen again. He didn't need a high paid manager to tell him that. Plus, Dan really wanted to get back to the servers and do something useful. The meeting droned on. Dan kept thinking how in order to be qualified for upper management you have to be able to speak confidently about subjects that you know nothing about.

The portable air conditioner arrived. The team worked all afternoon and on into the evening bringing up one server, testing it, bringing it on-line, and moving on to the next. Around 6:00 one of the workers stuck her head in Dan's office and said, "Hey Dan, the boss ordered pizza for us. It's in the break room. Come get some."

Dan wandered down to the break room. Most of the staff was already there. Some had already taken a piece of pizza and some were holding back trying to be polite.

Dan wanted to jump in, but he stopped himself. People had worked hard today and something needed to be said. None of the bosses were around. He didn't even know which one bought the pizza, so he thought the job of saying thank you fell to him. He wasn't afraid of public speaking. He had done it a lot, but impromptu speaking didn't come natural to him. Even so he went ahead.

Projecting his voice as much as he could he said, "Can I have your attention for a minute?" It took a few seconds for the crowd to turn their attention to him. "Go ahead and get your food while I talk. I know you can eat and listen at the same time. After seeing what you did today, I know you can do anything.

"I would guess that none of you thought you would have a day like this when you got up this morning. I know I didn't. When I first heard about the problem on the morning telecon my first thought was, 'I have no idea what I'm supposed to do.'

"My first glimmer of hope was when I got ahold of Mike on the phone. Mike, you might not think it was much, but I can't tell you how much it meant to me to have your eyes on the problem.

"After that you all jumped in. There is no way I can thank you individually, because it was like trying to follow ants round an ant hill. You were all over the problem and you wouldn't let go. I am proud of all of you.

"I am sure there are a few of you who, at least once in a while think you have a boring job. After today, I'm thinking that a boring job isn't such a bad thing.

"Go ahead and eat. There are a few systems we still need to activate tonight so the company can have normal operations in the morning. We are almost there. As you finish up, just know that what you have done today is appreciated, and I can't thank you enough."

He was very hungry. He hoped his speech didn't sound too cheesy, but it was the best he could do. He grabbed some pizza and a drink and collapsed into a breakroom chair. He wasn't really sitting with anyone, so he just listened to the conversations around him. Someone talked about having to get a last minute babysitter. Another about how the pizza was good, but she was so hungry that the boss could have bought cardboard and she would have eaten it. A man at the next table was going on about what a nightmare this whole day had been.

'A nightmare,' Dan thought. He hadn't thought about his dreams or his imaginary friend all day. The day was a nightmare to the man at the next table, but it wasn't for Dan. For Dan it was the first day in a week that he had been free of his nightmare. He thought about how strange that was. This guy and Dan had the same day. In fact, Dan's day was worse because he had to deal with management requesting status every few minutes. But even though both had the same day, the same problem, the same amount of work, the day was a nightmare for one of them but a relief for the other.

Dan sent the team home at 9:00. The company would be able to resume operations in the morning and he requested that a couple of the more experienced people come in early. He intended to be in early too. He made the 10:40 train to Elgin and got home well after midnight. He was relieved that Abbi didn't make an appearance on the train. He had spent the day without her and wanted to keep it that way.

He walked into a dark house. He had texted his mother about the whole ordeal. She knew how late he would be, and she wasn't about to stay up. He had eaten enough pizza that he wasn't hungry, so he went straight to bed. What seemed like minutes later he found himself on the porch of an old building. There were rocking chairs and when he looked out, he saw a dirt street.

He was going to step out into the street to see where he was when he heard Abbi's voice. "I am so sorry about last night. I didn't mean to make you late, but the dreams in the classroom were so interesting. I just lost track of time. I'm really sorry"

Dan wondered about that. The other Players he met were more serious, more focused. They were courteous to him, but they didn't talk very much. Abbi was different. She talked more, she seemed to enjoy her job more, but she was also more easily distracted. Was she the only Player like that, or were there others, but she happened to fall into the serious crowd? He wanted to ask but didn't think he should.

Instead, he asked, "Where am I?"

"You're in the old west. It's 1881," Abbi said happily.

"1881? So you can time travel?"

"No silly. It is a dream set made to look like 1881. I was told about your day and I thought that after a day like this you would appreciate being someplace where there are no computers," she said.

"You're right," Dan said.

"I should have asked a Tech to get me a long saloon dress. One with a derringer pistol in the garter on my leg," she laughed and continued, but she was wearing the same clothes as the other times.

"This is a famous place. Take a look down the street," she said,

Dan leaned over the rail and looked down the street. He saw a sign that said, "OK Corral."

"There was a gun fight here, I think," he said.

"Very good," Abbi said. "I'm told that we don't do as many western gun fights as we used to. Probably because Hollywood doesn't make as many westerns anymore. But I've seen some great dreams played out here. People wandering around while bullets are flying or they are part of the gang but can't get their gun out of its holster. Sometimes they just hide behind the watering trough trying to figure out what to do"

"Well, I'm glad you didn't actually bring me back in time." Dan said with a hint of sarcasm.

"Actually, we can move in more dimensions than you can, just not in time," Abbi said.

"How's that?" Dan asked.

"You can move around in three dimensions. We can move around in six. But time isn't one of them. We move through time just like you do. That's why you got up late this morning," Abbi said.

Dan was trying to understand. "I've read that physicists think there are ten or more dimensions, but it never made any sense to me."

"I don't know about the other four," Abbi said, "Actually, I don't really know about the six that I have. I just know that it works. Here, let me show you.

Abbi stepped down off the porch and onto the street below. Dan watched from the porch. She explained, "I'm here. Suppose I want to go there," as she pointed to a spot on the ground five feet away from her. "I could use three dimensions and walk there, or I could use six dimensions and get there faster."

With that she took one step and was at the spot five feet away. But it was odd. Dan blinked his eyes trying to understand what he was looking at. It was like there were two invisible door frames, one in each place and the moment Abbi entered one she exited the other. She went on to play around, standing halfway through the doors so Dan could see half of her in one place and half in the other. She flapped her arms and swayed back and forth. It was funny, but Dan was too confused to laugh.

Abbi climbed back onto the porch and sat in one of the rocking chairs. Dan sat in the other still feeling a little confused.

Abbi said, "I usually do dreams around the Chicago area, but sometimes they need me in faraway places and when they do, I can just take one step and I'm there. It is really fun. I hope this isn't too much for you. Oh, and I do have an assignment tonight, I hope you will come with. It's a onetime dream, not multiple like last night. I promise I will get you back on time."

It was the first time Dan felt like he had any choice in these dreams although he wasn't sure that he had any this time either. But as confused as he was, he did kind of like being with Abbi, so he agreed to go.

Abbi took his hand and they walked through the door in back of them. The next thing Dan knew he was on a football field. It was nighttime and the stadium lights were on.

"We're playing football?" Dan asked.

"No," Abbi answered. "We are in the marching band! Now here put this on and you will be in uniform."

Dan put on the coveralls, and Abbi handed him a trumpet.

"Hold it like this. We're all in the trumpet section," Abbi said as she showed him. "You are far enough down the line that the dreamer won't be able to see you very well. Just pretend to play and the Whisperer will take care of the rest."

"The what?" Dan asked.

"Not now. The dreamer's here," Abbi said as she lifted her trumpet up and pretended to play.

The dreamer was there. He stood in the line holding his own trumpet. He blew in it, but nothing came out. The line started to march forward. Dan awkwardly followed. The dreamer didn't know the drill; he didn't know what to do. There were dream Players near him who obviously knew what to do better than Dan. The dreamer would almost be catching on. He would start marching and suddenly the line would turn leaving him out in the open by himself. It is hard to say how long this went on, but eventually he disappeared, probably waking up and wondering where this stuff comes from.

Abbi turned to Dan. "That is it. I told you it was a one-off. Now you go back. You have to get up early. I'll see you soon."

Dan woke up. It was 4:00 AM. He knew the alarm was going to go off soon, but he still turned over and went back to sleep.

*   *   *

Getting in so late, it was a very short night. Even so he made an early train to be there before most people tried to start their computers. He did drift off on the train, but fortunately, Abbi left him alone.

When he arrived at work his two colleagues were already there and busy. He passed the break room. No one had cleaned up the pizza from the night before. He almost stopped but thought he had better check the systems first.

The morning was busy. There were the last of the less critical servers to start plus several lessons learned meetings where once again, management made sure this would never happen again. Dan tolerated the obvious. He thought about how it must make management feel better by saying obvious things. To Dan what they were saying was so apparent that a child would think of it.

It was noon when he remembered his appointment with the psychologist. He was tempted to cancel. After all, either he was crazy, or he wasn't. Going to the appointment wasn't going to change that. It might be better to be crazy and no one knows it than to be diagnosed and be on the record. But then he changed his mind and decided to go.

He found the email with all the paperwork to fill out. It was pages of check boxes. Dan wondered why a psychologist needed to know if there was cancer in his family or if he ever had a hernia. He checked no on all the boxes. No alcohol abuse. No allergies. No blood borne/infectious diseases. There was no check box for crazy.

Then he looked up the address. It was on Cermak Rd. in Cicero. Not the easiest place to get to by train, but he worked it out. He had thought of taking his car today but having to fight traffic and pay for parking made him change his mind. It was just too painful.

He had to take a different train than usual, but it looked the same as the others. Even so, he had to carefully watch the stops. He didn't know this route as well and if he missed the stop, he would miss the appointment. While he was riding, he was thinking that he was glad Abbi didn't whisk him away or he would definitely miss his stop.

He made it to the psychologist's office with time to spare. It was on the top floor of an older three-story building. He checked in and sat down. There was nothing to do so he took out his phone to check messages or look at whatever to pass the time. He heard people talking and moving around. He noticed that the office was set up so that the entrance and the exit were two different doors. That is, so that people coming in would never see people leaving and the other way around.

The office door opened. "Mr. Andersen?"

Dan got up and was escorted to an office by a nice lady. It was probably the voice he talked to a couple of days before. She brought him in and announced, "This is Mr. Andersen." She then left and closed the door behind her.

"Hello, Mr. Andersen. Come in. I am Dr. Keller. Have a seat.

Dr. Keller was sitting at her desk, but she motioned for Dan to sit in a stuffed fabric chair in the middle of the room. There were two opposing chairs with a coffee table in the middle.

"Give me just a minute," Dr. Keller said, as she finished some kind of paperwork.

Dan sat down. He wasn't really facing the doctor, but he could see out of the corner of his eye that she was a thin, middle aged woman. She had shoulder length auburn hair that very likely had some help keeping its color. She was dressed professionally in a navy blue business suit, with a knee length skirt, jacket, and a white blouse.

It was awkward to wait. Dan wanted to pull his phone out, but he didn't think that would have been appropriate. He looked at the coffee table. It was nearly empty except for a brochure of some kind that was facing away from him. Dan didn't think it would be appropriate to pick it up to read either, but it was sitting in plain sight.

He thought back to a college internship he had with a trucking company. He had a good boss, but a boss that tried a little too hard to mentor him. He would call Dan into his office and give him long speeches on how business should run. Dan would try to look interested, but he was actually practicing reading the boss's papers upside down. It was never anything personal or private, but Dan found reading upside down to be a way of staying entertained.

He usually got stuck on a word or two, but he found this brochure easy to read upside down:

Never Alone Foundation
A friend to those who are alone
in the last years of their life.
Too many people have no one and in the last days
of their life they have no companion to walk with
them and care for them
The Never Alone Foundation is here to ensure no
one is left alone.

Dan wondered if it was a charity the doctor supported, or if some earlier patient had left it behind.

Dr. Keller joined him by sitting in the other chair.

"Mr. Andersen, can I call you Daniel or Dan?"

"Dan is OK."

"So, Dan, what brings you here? The rep from Protectcare said you were having nightmares"

"I've been having dreams," Dan said. "But they aren't nightmares. In fact most of them are rather pleasant. But they are different than anything I've ever experienced. They are as real as you and me sitting here. I remember all of them like I remember things when I am awake."

Dan told Dr. Keller the events of many of the dreams. He told her about Abbi and how she was giving him tours of dreams. He tried to explain about dream Players and how dreams are made, but he didn't think his explanation came out very clear.

Dr. Keller asked him about stress at work, about his family, and about living with his mother. They talked about Dan's feelings about losing his dad not too many years ago. She continually asked him what he thought or how he felt about everything. Dan didn't think that was helpful at all. He was hoping she would offer advice, not try to get him to make his own.

The hour went by very quickly. Dr. Keller told him that he was experiencing vivid dreams. She said that often they happen when people are going through difficult or painful events in life, such as losing a loved one, job or money pressures, or anything that can lead to feelings of stress or anxiety. Dan didn't think the pressures at work were that bad, and it had been years since he lost his father, but he didn't have any other explanation.

She assured him that he wasn't insane and that if they could work through the causes of the dreams, the dreams would no longer be needed and would stop. She gave him some tips to try to create a healthier work-life balance and tried to get him to commit to consistent exercise. She also suggested taking a natural sleep aid like valerian root or melatonin. They agreed to schedule another appointment for the following Monday.

'Natural sleep aids,' Dan thought as he left the building. 'I was hoping she would have something stronger. The pharmaceutical companies must be working on something. Maybe they have an anti-Abbi pill, or how about a dream dissolver salve. How about an anti-Player potion.' He laughed quietly at the thought of his poetic potions.

As he waited for the bus, he thought about how he wasn't so sure the doctor was going to be able to help him at all. The dreams seemed too real to be talked away. Still, she seemed to have an understanding and really, he had no other options.

Dan was home early enough to have dinner with his mother. He decided that now that he had actually seen a psychologist, he needed to tell her. At least he needed to tell her something. It would be too awkward if she found out later even a long time later. He told her that he was under a lot of pressure from work, that it was causing strange dreams, so he contacted the company's EAP program and left it at that.

He went to bed and soon found himself on the top of a mountain. It was bright and sunny. There were snowcapped mountains all around. Even though there was snow all around it wasn't cold. It was stunningly beautiful. Dan had the thought of taking a picture. He reached into his pocket and pulled out his cell phone, but soon realized that it wasn't his cell phone. It was a prop. The Dream Technicians must have put it there. Dan felt silly. Of course he wouldn't be able to take a picture in a dream, and if he did it would disappear as soon as he woke up.

He heard a voice. "Did they tell you that you are crazy?" It was Abbi.

Dan turned to look at her. She had a flirtatious smile on her face.

"No," Dan replied. "Evidently you are the result of pressure at work and grieving over the loss of my father five years ago."

"I didn't know about your father," Abbi said. "I'm sorry"

"He died of a heart attack five years ago," Dan said. "I really don't think he is causing you to be here. But the doctor thinks you may be caused by other pressures in my life. You seem to know how work has been lately"

"He doesn't know what he's talking about." Abbi said.

Dan replied, "He is a she. Dr. Margret Keller, Cognitive Psychologist."

Abbi's expression changed. She looked like she saw a ghost or like she had just opened a cabinet and found that it was full of snakes."

"What's wrong?" Dan asked.

There was fear in Abbi's voice. "I, I don't know. There was something about that name. I don't know why. I..." She couldn't speak any more.

Dan tried to get her to talk but she wouldn't. She had tears in her eyes.

She choked out the words, "I'm sorry."

Dan found himself in his bed. It was 11:00 PM. He wondered what had just happened. Dream Players were always in control. They shouldn't be afraid of anything. He fell back asleep for the rest of the night.

Chapter 4
The Last Dream

The next day on the train Dan was thinking about the night before. It was short, but so different than the other nights. It could be that his subconscious made Abbi afraid of Dr. Keller. After all, she could make Abbi go away. It was very confusing.

He thought about the beauty of the mountains. He had seen scenes like that on television, but never in person. To see them in person would mean hiking in tough conditions to finally make it to the pinnacle of the mountain where it is all worth it. In the dream he was just there, and it was spectacular. He wished the phone in his pocket hadn't been a prop. Then he could look at the pictures and know if it was real or not. In fact, he could take a picture of Abbi and prove that she was real.

'Take a picture of Abbi,' he thought. He wished he had a picture of Abbi. Not only to prove she was real, and not only to prove that he wasn't crazy, but also because, well, because he wished he had her picture. Then he had a new thought. He waited until he was in the relative quiet of his office, looked up the non-emergency number of the Elgin Police Department, and called the number.

"Elgin Police Department, how may I direct your call?" a voice said.

"Can you connect me to your sketch artist?" Dan asked.

The voice replied, "Do you have a name or department number?"

Dan sighed. "Can you connect me to the sergeant or whoever is in charge?"

There were some clicks and a phone ringing sound. "This is Sargent Marc Bradford. How can I help you?"

Dan suddenly realized that he couldn't tell the real story, but he needed to say something. "Do you have a sketch artist I could talk to? I have a friend who just left the country, and I don't have a picture of her, so I wanted to get a sketch." Dan winced at how bad his story sounded.

Sargent Bradford ignored the silliness and replied, "We use a computer system that is for official use only. If we need a live artist, we borrow one from the Chicago P.D. I don't know if they can help you or not, but I can give you the phone number."

Dan took the phone number but decided to try to think of a better story this time. Later in the day he made the next call.

"Chicago Police Department, can I help you?" a voice said.

"My name is Dan Andersen. I need to have a sketch made of someone that saved my life. She disappeared before I could thank her or even get her name. I was hoping to post it on-line to thank her for caring so much, and maybe find out who she is." Dan felt better about this lie.

The voice answered, "I'm sorry. We can only do sketches in connection with an investigation."

Dan replied, "OK, I understand."

He was about to hang up when the voice continued, "I do have a suggestion for you, if you're interested"

"What's that?" Dan answered.

"Our best sketch artist retired a couple years ago. Now he does freelance art out of his home. We bring him in as a consultant occasionally. You might be able to hire him. I don't know what he would charge, but it might be worth a call."

Dan took down the name and number and called immediately.

"Hello," a voice answered.

"Is this Bob Weber?" Dan asked. "My name is Dan Anderson. I was given your number by the Chicago Police Department. I need to have a police sketch made and I was hoping you could help."

"I've done a few of them in my time," Bob said. "Are you the witness?"

It took Dan a second to realize what he was asking. "Yes. I'm the one who knows what she looks like."

"I see," Bob said. "What do you intend to use this sketch for?"

Dan couldn't lie again. "Look. You'll probably think I'm crazy, but I've been having these dreams. The same girl shows up in all of them. I'm trying to deal with it, and I think that if I had a picture of her, it would help me work through it."

Bob answered, "Well, son, I can try to make your sketch. I would charge you the same fee I charge the CPD, $75.00 per hour. I charge them for transportation, but we can do this at my house, so you wouldn't have to pay for that. But let me warn you. The odds are against us getting a good sketch. Believe it or not I've tried to draw dream people before. The dreamers are so confident that they know what the person in their dream looks like until they go to describe them. Then they find that there isn't nearly as much detail as they thought.

"I have to try," Dan said. "Put me down for two hours."

"I can usually finish a sketch in less than an hour, and I don't want to take your money. I'll block out two hours for you, but you only need to pay for what it takes."

"Great. When can we meet and where do you live?" Dan said.

"Let's see. I'm tied up all day tomorrow. Would Saturday be OK with you?" Bob said.

"Yes. Any time. The sooner the better. Where do you live?"

"I live in Logan Square." He gave the address. "One o'clock in the afternoon will be best for me."

Dan agreed. He hung up and went back to work. He wasn't sure how having a sketch would help, but he believed it was necessary. Maybe if he showed Dr. Keller she would understand how real the dreams seemed to be to him.

He got home at a reasonable time, watched some TV and went to bed. The next thing he knew he was back on the serene dock with the beautiful lake. He sat on the bench with a thatched roof above him. He took a few minutes to enjoy the place knowing that Abbi would be there soon.

It took longer than he expected, but she walked down the dock and sat next to him.

"Are you OK?" Dan asked. The question was genuine, but he still thought it was strange that he cared about an imaginary friend.

"I'm better," Abbi said. "I don't know what came over me. I've never heard that name before, but hearing it was like, well, walking up to a curtain and parting it just a little to peek through and seeing a holocaust on the other side. I felt like I was kidnapped and beaten. Tremendous pain. I was thrown in the ocean, then picked up by a bird. A large noisy bird. Then I was attacked by snakes. Snakes in my mouth and nose and arms. It was only for a second, but it was so intense.

"I thought about it a lot since then. I might be remembering a dream that I was in that went bad. It does happen. I don't remember one like that, but it is the kind of thing we put in dreams, and I have been in some that didn't work out very well at all. Maybe it was someone with a similar name?"

Dan just listened. He was thinking that an imaginary person would look at a psychologist as someone who would kidnap them and throw them in the ocean. They wouldn't go willingly. Maybe he could ask Dr. Keller about it.

Realizing it was quiet, Dan said, "Do you have an assignment tonight?"

Abbi answered, "No. The Maker thought I should rest a little more. I should go back to work tomorrow."

"The Maker?" Dan asked. "Who is that?"

"He is the Dream Maker," Abbi said. "We all work for him"

"Yes, you told me that before, but who or what is he?" Dan asked.

"All dreams come from him," Abbi said.

"So, he's the author of all my dreams?" Dan said.

"The author, yes, but he also lets us improvise a lot," Abbi said. "Some dreams he writes himself and others he allows the Dream Masters to do what they want. Sometimes the Dream Masters just let us adlib. Those can get crazy."

Abbi had a slight grin as if she were remembering a particularly crazy dream.

"I'll bet the dreams where you can improvise are the best," Dan said.

"Oh no. The dream maker's dreams are the best. Everyone works their hardest to make sure everything is perfect. The Technicians spend weeks getting everything just right, so the Whisperers hardly have anything to do, and the Erasers are barely needed at all," Abbi said.

"The who? The what?" Dan said.

Abbi took a deep breath and started to explain. "Dreams are made by a group of Players with special skills. For instance, I am a Dream Player. I play parts in dreams. People see me. You might consider me a minor Player. I am usually in a crowd, or sitting with others round a table, or like you and I did in the elevator. There are other Dream Players that we call Dream Masters. They organize and plan the dreams. They are better at playing the main role, but I like being off to the side. That way I can watch everything that is happening and see the dreamer's reaction.

"Then there are the Dream Technicians. There are lots of different skills among the Techs. I suppose they specialize like we do, but I never really paid attention. Anyway, there are Techs who build the sets, others who make all the mechanical things work, and others that make costumes and disguises. They are very smart, but you never see them in your dream. They are always in the background.

"There are also Dream Whisperers. They whisper thoughts into your brain to make you think things are different than they are. For instance, have you ever had a dream where you knew you were someplace, but nothing looked like the place really looks. Maybe in your dream you're at your grandmother's house. You know you're at your grandmother's house, but it doesn't look like you know how the place looks. It is because the Whisperer told you it was your grandmother's house. Sometimes a dream is too complicated, and it needs some help. Sometimes we run out of time and use a set from someone else's dream, but the Whisperer makes you think it is the real place.

"Finally, there is the Dream Erasers. Most people don't remember their dreams. They shouldn't. If they did, they would start to confuse their dream world with their waking world. One word or one touch from the Dream Eraser and your dream starts to fade. Sometimes people wake up before the Eraser is finished and they remember their dreams. Lots of times the Eraser touches the dreamer before the dream is over, so they remember the last little bit.

"Some people try real hard to defeat the Eraser so they can analyze their dreams, but they can only do so much. At the same time, I think the Erasers have an odd sense of humor. If a Dreamer has a particularly strange or interesting dream, they might decide to hardly erase any of it. They enjoyed the dream, so they let the Dreamer keep it so they can enjoy it too. Or at least it seems that way. I don't know."

Dan and Abbi sat on the dock and talked for what seemed like hours. Abbi told Dan that she didn't want to repeat her mistake of making him oversleep, so finally she said goodbye and Dan woke up in his bed. Seconds later his alarm went off and it was time to get up.

Dan went through his normal morning routine and arrived at work on time. The office had returned to normal. There were the normal pressures of everyday work, but nothing unusual. He went through the day feeling really good. It was as if he had had a very good date the night before. When he was in college he dated once in a while, but when he left school, it seemed that dating stayed behind. In fact, lately it was worse because work had pretty much replaced his social life.

He finished his day and left work only a little late. He was able to have dinner with his mother, watch a little TV and off to bed. Normally he wouldn't go to bed that early on a Friday night, but for the first time in over a week he was actually looking forward to it.

He fell asleep and moments later found himself in an open place. Everything was light blue. There were no walls, no sky, no ground, and no horizon. It was as if he were in a giant blue bubble. Immediately, Abbi appeared as if she had walked through one of her invisible doors.

"Sorry," she said, "We can't do anything together tonight. We are setting up for a really important dream tomorrow night and they need my help. The Maker said that you can't help with the setup, but you can come to the dream tomorrow, so go to bed early if you can. See you tomorrow."

Dan woke up. He looked at the clock. He had been in bed for 10 minutes. 'Wow,' Dan thought. 'I've been brushed off by an imaginary woman. Imaginary women are just like real women.' Dan fell back asleep.

*   *   *

The next morning was Saturday. It was the day he was to meet with the sketch artist. He took his time in the morning then started out on the hour drive to Logan Square. He never liked to drive downtown for work. The traffic was always horrible and the parking nearly impossible. But a Saturday driving to an outer neighborhood wasn't so bad.

He drove it in forty five minutes, but still had problems finding a place to park. All the streets were lined on both sides with parked cars. There were no driveways or garages. Everyone who had a car left it on the street. He drove past the artist's home and found a parking place two blocks away.

The artist lived in a three story red brick bungalow. Each floor was a dwelling, and the artist lived on the third floor. Dan climbed a set of concrete steps and looked at the three mailboxes by the door. The one on the right said, "Weber." He pressed the button by the mailbox. A few seconds later he heard a buzzing sound and he was able to open the door.

He climbed the two flights of stairs and found himself in a dark alcove. Seconds later a door opened. In the doorway was an older man wearing jeans, a plaid shirt, with suspenders.

"You're Dan Andersen?" the man said.

Dan nodded.

"I'm Bob Weber. Welcome."

Bob escorted him through a dining area and into a back bedroom that he had set up as an art studio. The walls were covered with paintings and sketches. He had an easel set up in the middle of the room with a stool behind it. In front of it was an overstuffed chair, where his models sit while they are being painted.

"So, you want me to sketch a lady you saw in your dreams. Do you still remember her?" Bob asked.

"Oh, yes," Dan answered. "I saw her last night, although only for a few minutes. But the night before we sat and talked for hours."

"You did huh," Bob said under his breath. Then in a stronger voice, "Here is how we will try to work this. I have my old trait book. We will start by going through and picking the shape of the woman's head, her hair, nose and so forth. I'll put them into a rough sketch. As I go, I'll keep asking you questions, and you can feel free to point out things that need to change. I've done this many times before. You won't offend me if you see something wrong."

Over the next hour the two men worked together. Dan was impressed by how Bob knew exactly the right questions to ask. His years of experience showed. At the same time Bob was amazed at how much detail Dan remembered. He never expected that. It was as if he were describing a wife or a longtime girlfriend.

At the end of the hour Bob had completed the sketch. He held it up and said to Dan, "The hour is up. We have a pretty good sketch. If I were consulting for CPD this is all they would want. They would pay me and send me home. But I can offer you a little more. You see from my walls that I am an artist, or at least I am trying to be. You offered to pay for two hours. If you want to hire me for that second hour I can make you a more life-like color version."

"Absolutely," Dan said. "I would love to have that. But now she needs to have more of a playful smile and more of a cagey expression on her face"

"Hmm," Bob grunted, "I'll see what I can do."

Then over the next hour he created a life-like portrait of Abbi. By the time he was done anyone who looked at the portrait would have thought that Abbi sat in the overstuffed chair the whole time while he worked.

Dan left and walked to his car. For the longest time he sat in the car looking at the portrait. After a while he pulled out his phone and took a picture of it. If he couldn't do it in a dream, he was going to do it now.

He wondered how he could have imagined that much detail. He must have seen her someplace and forgot. Forgot? It might be possible to see her in passing and forget, but what about her personality? Did he imagine that too? Did he experience it and forget? It was hard to think about. Every time he tried, he hit a dead end.

He drove home and put the picture in the brief case he brings to work. He wanted to show his mother, but he didn't want to make up a story to go with it. He wanted to frame it and put it on the wall, but that would mean even more explaining. Still, he was happy to have it and to him it was money well spent. He had dinner with his mother and went to bed as early as he could without having to make up an excuse.

* * *

It felt like an instant later that he was in a magnificent place. It was a wide open floor and all around it looked like the courtyard of a Spanish palace. There were stucco arches with flowering vines crawling up them. Above the arches were extravagant balconies with wrought iron rails. Dan looked up and saw that the room was lit by Crystal chandeliers. Above the chandeliers was a terra-cotta ceiling. It was all incredibly detailed, not like the sets he had seen in other dreams.

There were Dream Players starting to arrive and milling around. They were all well-dressed. The men all wore a jacket and tie. A few men were in some kind of a military uniform. They were across the floor, so Dan couldn't see them well. The women all wore dresses.

Dan saw Abbi across the floor. She was talking to one of the Dream Players. He walked over and greeted her.

Abbi saw Dan and said, "Isn't it beautiful?"

"Where are we?" Dan asked.

Abbi answered, "You are in the Aragon Ballroom in Chicago. It is the most beautiful ballroom in the world! Its 1944 and a dance is about to begin. Now, put this on so you fit in."

Abbi handed Dan a bundle of cloth that unfolded into another pair of coveralls.

As Dan put on the coveralls, he looked around some more. At one end of the room was a stage and across the front of the stage was a banner that said "Harry James." He wondered if maybe that was the name of the dreamer. Dream Players started to populate the stage, each wearing a gaudy tuxedo and each carrying an instrument.

The Dream Maker

The band started to play, and the Dream Players started to dance. Dan had seen scenes like this before in old World War II movies. One song ended and another started, and the dancing continued. The ballroom was very crowded with dancing Dream Players.

Dan was starting to wonder if maybe this was a party for Dream Players and not someone's dream at all. But at that moment he noticed a very old lady standing at one end of the dance floor. She was wearing a robe, or it could have been a hospital gown. Her hair was white and thinning. She seemed to have trouble standing. She was hunched over. Her quivering hands were held out in front of her as if she were holding an invisible walker.

Dan turned and looked at Abbi to ask if this was the dreamer.

Abbi answered softly, "Yes. It is her last dream."

Dan looked back toward the lady. The old lady was gone. Instead, there was a young energetic girl wearing a red party dress. She had all the beauty of youth. Her arms crossed with her hands on opposite upper arms while she swayed and swirled and danced to the music. She had a look of paradise on her face. She was young again and in the only place in any time she wanted to be.

Dan didn't see any spotlights, yet somehow where she was, was lit brighter than the rest of the room. The song ended and the next one began. It started with an orchestra introduction and a trumpet solo that was loud and clear. During the solo the girl stopped dancing. She dropped her hands to her side and stared straight ahead in disbelief.

There across the room was a young man in an Army uniform. He had a smile on his face as he confidently walked toward her. One arm raised as if inviting her to dance with him.

Abbi whispered to Dan, "That's her husband. He has been gone eighteen years."

As the two came close together a woman's voice started to sing from the orchestra,

> *Never thought that you would be*
> *standing here so close to me*
> *there's so much I feel that I should say*
> *but words can wait until some other day*
>
> *Kiss me once, then kiss me twice*
> *Then kiss me once again*
> *It's been a long, long time...*

The two started to dance. Everyone else in the room stopped dancing. They moved to the side to watch.

Dan looked over at Abbi. She had tears in her eyes. She had trouble speaking, but managed to say, "This is the day they met. For the rest of her life, she would tell people 'I was 20 years old on that day, but it was the first day of my life.'"

The song ended and the couple kissed. There was silence for a short period before the band started playing again. Now the Dream Players join in and the dance floor was a blur of swirling couples. The dancing continued for hours, but to the girl in the red party dress it could have continued forever.

Finally the band started playing a different melody. It wasn't dance music. It had the sound of the 1940's, but it had a more dramatic tone to it. The crowd moved aside to form a long aisle down the middle of the room. The couple stood at one end. The man put his arm around her in a reassuring way.

At the other end of the aisle a figure moved from dark into the light. Dan could see him, but he couldn't describe him. It was almost like he was looking at a blurred image, but he wasn't. The one part that was clear was the look on his face. He was smiling. He looked happy.

Dan glanced at the other Dream Players in the room, and they looked happy too. To him that was unusual. Usually there was no emotion on Dream Player's faces unless they were acting in someone's dreams. That is of course except for Abbi who always has all kinds of emotions.

Abbi whispered to Dan, "That's the Dream Maker."

The moment was intense with the Dream Maker facing the couple. He then raised his arms and gestured for them to come to him. The man escorted the girl forward, as the

Dream Maker walked toward them. They met in the middle. The Dream Maker gave the girl a big hug while the man stood to the side. They all walked together to the end of the aisle and into the darkness.

There was a long silence. All the Dream Players on the dance floor stood still gazing into the dark. Dan couldn't see their faces, but he felt a sadness. Were they sad because The Maker had left or because the woman was gone? He couldn't tell.

Before Dan had a chance to think any more about it there was a loud, clear, note from a trumpet. It was the orchestra leader. He was starting a new tune. At the end of the long note the orchestra started to play. But this music was different. Dan had never heard anything like it. Many of the Players in the orchestra had put down their 1940's instruments and were playing instruments that Dan had never seen before.

The Dream Players started dancing again. They were laughing and having fun. They kept the party going even though the dream had ended. But now they were doing different dances. The swing dances were for the dream, now the Players danced their own way.

Dan could see different dances in different areas of the dance floor. Sometimes a Player would solo dance while others circled around and cheered. Others were more formal. Abbi was at the end of a long line dance. As she swept by she grabbed Dan by the hand and pulled him in.

Dan circled trying to keep up. He was running in a circle, but it felt like the room was spinning around him. He felt so awkward that he started to think it was his own bad dream. Abbi didn't care. She was caught up in the moment as she whirled around the dance floor.

It didn't stop. Abbi would see another group of dancers and she would jump in. She had to try and each time she did she dragged Dan with. Dan tried to keep up, but it was futile. The best he could do is hold on and do his best to fake it.

Dan woke up. It was 10:30 AM. It was a good thing that this dream happened on a Saturday night.

Chapter 5
The Chase

That morning it took Dan a long time to get going. He pretty much had breakfast for lunch. He had promised his mother that he would fix the leaking kitchen sink and that took the rest of the day. He was generally good at fixing things, but plumbing was never fun and it always took longer than he thought.

The day flew by and is seemed like no time before it was time to go to bed again. Dan wasn't sure he was ready for another dream. Especially after the spectacle of the night before. But tomorrow was a workday, and he needed to rest. He had found that even though he was active all night he was never tired the next day. After all, he was sleeping the whole time.

Reluctantly Dan went to bed. The next thing he knew he was back on the dock, sitting on the wooden bench. The peaceful lake stretched out in front of him with beautiful deep woods beyond. Abbi was already there. She was slightly in back of him leaning against a rail.

"What did you think of last night?" she said. "It was so exciting."

"I'm still processing it." Dan said. "You said that was her last dream. So, after that she died?"

"It was the end of her life on Earth," Abbi said. "I don't really know at that moment whether her life had ended or if it was about to end, but it doesn't matter. The Maker gave her one last dream, and what a wonderful dream it was.

"She got to go with the Dream Maker right away. Not everyone does. Some people wake up. It is still the end of their life and they will never have another dream, but I think the Dream Maker lets them wake up so they can say goodbye to their loved ones. The last dream gives them a burst of energy, so they can enjoy being with their family and friends for a little while before they have to leave."

"Does everyone get a last dream?" Dan asked.

"No. Not everyone. I don't know why some people do and some don't. I just know that when someone gets a last dream we do our absolute best to make it the best dream we can, the best dream of their life," Abbi said.

"It was more than just a dream," Dan said. "The Dream Players kept the party going into the night. They seemed so happy."

"They were happy. They were happy to see Dorothy, that was her name, go with the Dream Maker. There is nothing better than being with the Dream Maker," Abbi said. "Besides, they had been in her dreams for almost one hundred years. That's about how old she was. They knew her and wanted the best for her. It might seem odd, but they were happy and sad at the same time. They were happy that she was with The Maker, but they were sad to see her go."

"Well, I didn't know that Dream Players could be so much fun. They seem so serious and gloomy all the rest of the time," Dan said.

"Everyone needs to let loose sometimes, and Dream Players are no different. You probably couldn't tell, but there were Technicians, Whisperers, and Erasers on the dance floor last night too," Abbi responded.

Dan rolled his head and said, "You're right. It was all a blur."

Abbi looked at Dan. "You've asked me so many questions about last night, now I have one for you."

"Shoot," Dan replied.

"How many left feet do you have?" Abbi giggled.

Dan sighed, "Alright I'm not a dancer."

"Maybe you need to take some lessons," Abbi said still half laughing.

"They tried to teach me in middle school," He said. "They failed miserably"

Abbi giggled some more.

"We have to get going," Abbi said. "I have an assignment tonight."

She motioned for Dan to get up. They walked together to the end of the pier and through an invisible door. Dan found himself back in the busy main corridor. Technicians and Players were bustling back and forth getting set up to stage their next dream.

As they walked, Abbi said, "Are you going to see that doctor again tomorrow?

"Yes, I have an appointment," Dan answered.

"Be careful. I still don't know why so much fear came over me, but something isn't right," Abbi said in a serious tone.

"I'll be careful," Dan said. He didn't want to trigger Abbi again, but he still had the thought that his subconscious knows that Dr. Keller has the power to make Abbi go away, so it has her act up if her name is mentioned. It was the only explanation that made sense.

They turned a corner and walked through a door. They were in the middle of a deserted city street. It was dark and didn't look like a very good neighborhood.

"Where are we?" Dan asked.

"I don't know for sure," Abbi answered. "Some generic city. Someplace where most people don't really want to be. Here put this on."

Abbi handed Dan a bundle and some odd looking shoes.

Dan knew the drill. They looked like coveralls to him, but the Technicians or maybe it's the Whisperers can make the dreamer see him wearing whatever they want when he has them on. The Players always wore actual costumes, but Dan guessed it was easier for them to give him generic coveralls.

"What will I be dressed as?" Dan asked, thinking he might be a street gang member.

"We will both be invisible," Abby answered. "The dreamer won't be able to see us at all."

"So, what are we going to be doing?" Dan asked.

"Tonight, we are chasing people," Abbi said. "I'll go first and show you, then you can take a turn."

Dan barely understood what Abbi was talking about. Abbi had him stand off to the side where he could watch. Abbi walked back a few yards. Shortly after that a dreamer appeared. It was a woman in her mid-forties. She stood in the middle of the street looking around. Abbi started lifting and dropping her feet as if she were marching in place. The special shoes on her feet made a distinctive clomping sound. At first it was very slow, clomp, clomp, clomp, clomp.

The woman looked around; sure that someone or something was coming toward her. She started to walk down the street, moving slowly, afraid to give eye contact to the thing in back of her. She was walking, but the Technicians had rigged the street so that she didn't actually go anywhere. Dan could stand in one place and watch the whole thing.

Abbi picked up the tempo and stomped a little harder as if the thing was getting closer.

The woman broke into a full out run, and Abbi increased the tempo as if the hideous thing chasing her was faster than she was. She ran and ran until some Dream Player, possibly a Dream Master, yelled for Abbi to stop. It was obvious the dreamer couldn't hear the call.

The woman stopped running. Her heart was pounding as she nervously stopped. She looked around but was afraid to look in the direction of the thing.

Just then another Player, Dan thought an Eraser, came up to her, touched her and she disappeared.

"OK it's your turn," Abbi called to Dan. "Come over here."

Dan walked over.

Abbi put a hand on each of his arms and placed him in the middle of the street. Dan looked ahead. It was a different street. Still kind of dingy, but maybe a different city or town. He guessed that the Technicians customized the set for each dreamer.

Abbi gave him a briefing. "You don't have to go anyplace, just march in place. March just a little faster than the dreamer. With a little practice you can make the footstep sound get louder, so the dreamer thinks you are getting closer. Don't be afraid to try. Both the Whisperer and the Eraser know it is your first time, so they will fix anything that goes wrong."

Moments later the dreamer appeared. This time it was a young man, maybe even a teenager. Dan started clomping, and the boy started running. Dan clomped faster and the boy ran faster. At one point the boy fell, looking like a quivering mass on the ground, but then he got up and pushed on, always fighting the urge to look back at whoever or whatever was chasing him.

Abbi and Dan continued to take turns being the chaser. Dan lost count of how many people they chased that night. Each one had their own scene. Some in the city, some in the woods, a few were even in a school hallway. Some were brave and faced their aggressor, but most were lungs on fire desperately trying to get away.

There was one that must have been into martial arts or worked in some field like law enforcement, because he was fearless. It was later in the night and Dan felt like he was getting the chasing thing down. He started marching in place making the clomp, clomp sound. But the dreamer didn't run. He turned and stared back looking for his attacker. Dan hoped that the invisible suit was working because it looked like the man was ready for a fight.

The Dreamer stopped and looked around. He listened intently as if he were hunting in the woods, listening to his prey rustlings in the bushes. Dan stopped marching and there was dead silence. But then he moved his left foot just a little and a soft clomp came out. It was enough for the Dreamer. He hurled himself toward Dan. Dan dove out of the way and the man disappeared.

In the break between Dreamers, Dan asked Abbi about it. She explained that Dan's theory about him being a police officer might be right, but it could be that The Maker asked the Dream Master to help the Dreamer build confidence. The Master might have designed the dream so that the Dreamer could win.

Dan woke up. It was 5:00 AM. He rolled over in bed knowing that he could still get another hour of sleep.

* * *

Work the next day was normal. As usual it was filled with meetings, phone calls and emails. Even though he was busy, the scenes of the night before kept coming back to him. If he found a private moment, he would pull out his phone and look at the drawing of Abbi.

He had the appointment with Dr. Keller later in the afternoon. He started wondering if he should go. She had the power to make Abbi go away, but Dan wasn't sure he wanted Abbi to go away. Maybe it was OK to have an imaginary friend. It didn't hurt anyone. He was still able to function when he was awake. It wasn't like some addiction that ruined everyone's life. It was only his life, and it wasn't unpleasant at all.

He continued to argue with himself. It isn't normal. People don't live like this. Maybe lots of others live like this, and just don't tell anyone. Maybe he was abnormal before this and having a dream life is normal. No. He needed to see the doctor and he needed to get to the bottom of this! He was going to the appointment. He left work early enough to take the Burlington Northern train to Cicero.

He barely made it to the appointment on time. There was no time in the waiting room. He was glad about that. He didn't want to have time to think. Just go.

Dr. Keller started off, "Hello Dan. "It's good to see you. How have you been the last few days?"

"About the same," Dan answered. "I am still having the dreams."

"Tell me about them," Dr. Keller said.

Dan hesitated. Telling her about the 'last dream' seemed kind of personal. It almost seemed disrespectful to Dorothy. Then the arguments in his head started again. Dorothy isn't real. There is no Dorothy. You can't be disrespectful to her. It still didn't seem right, so he started to tell the doctor about people being chased.

Dan started off, "Last night, people were being chased. There were lots of them, but only one at a time, and each one was different."

Dr. Keller replied, "Dreams about being chased are some of the most common dreams. Usually, they mean that you are anxious about something. You might be experiencing heightened or ongoing stress, you could be worried about an upcoming event, or overwhelmed with responsibilities. You might be wishing to avoid something you'd rather not face."

Dan was thinking, "Abbi is right. These people don't know squat about dreams."

Dan cut her off. "No, you don't understand. I wasn't being chased. I was making noises that made other people dream that they were being chased. I was invisible, but I was wearing special shoes that made a clomping sound. I would make the sound, people would hear it, and they would think they are being chased. When they ran, I would increase the frequency and make it louder, so they would think I was gaining on them.

"We chased many different people. I lost count of how many. But the scene, the location changed for each one. Some were in city streets, some in the halls of a building. "

"You were busy," Dr. Keller said.

"Actually, Abbi and I took turns. That made it easier," Dan said.

"Abbi," Dr. Keller said, "The girl you talked about last time. So, she is still in your dreams?"

"Oh yes, every one of them," Dan said, "That's part of the problem. She seems so real. It is hard for me to believe that she isn't. When I wake up it is no different than when I leave here. She is just as real as you are."

"That is interesting. But in reality, she is not just as real as people. You just think she is," Dr. Keller said.

"I tell myself that, but I don't believe it," Dan said as he started to pick up his briefcase.

Dan rummaged around inside his brief case and pulled out the drawing of Abbi.

"If I just think she is real, how could I have described this?" Dan said as he handed the drawing to Dr. Keller.

Dr. Keller stared at the picture. A look of horror came across her face. Dan was distracted trying to stuff things back into his brief case and didn't notice.

Dr. Keller held the picture and half staggered to her desk in back of Dan where she couldn't be seen. She swallowed and took a deep breath. Then her look of horror changed to a look of anger. She tried to hide her anger as she returned to her chair across from Dan.

"Where did you get this?" she asked, as she handed the picture back.

Dan explained about hiring an artist.

Dr. Keller continued, "I agree that you couldn't imagine this much detail, but I believe it is because you have seen this lady someplace." Sternly, "Where?"

Dan insisted that he had never seen her, but Dr. Keller persisted, "You have. Think. At your work? On the train? In a restaurant? In a hospital? Where?"

Dan told her that he had not, and that he hadn't even been to a hospital in years. Dr. Keller persisted. She acted more like she was interrogating a prisoner than conducting a counseling session.

Dan was in his own world. He was on the defensive and couldn't notice that Dr. Keller had a sound of desperation in her voice.

The grilling went on for half an hour. Dan was glad when the session was over so he could get out of there.

After he left, Dr. Keller sat at her desk trying to recover. A few minutes later she got up and locked the office door. Then she picked up the phone.

A man's voice on the other end answered, "Hello."

"This is Margret. We have a problem," she said.

"What's that?"

"The snoop is alive," she said.

The voice sounded concerned, "Are you sure? Have you seen her?"

"No," she replied

"Then how do you know she is alive?" he asked.

"I know you will think this is crazy, but I have a patient who has been having vivid dreams," Margret said. "Those are dreams that seem real and can be remembered in detail. He told me that there was the same girl in every dream. I didn't think much of it. That happens. But he was so sure that he went out and hired a sketch artist to draw the girl in his dreams. They made a sketch from his description, and, I'm telling you, it is her."

The voice sounded firm, "That's not possible."

"It is if he has seen her. That is if he has seen her often and recently," She said.

"No," the voice said.

"Then how do you explain the picture. I tell you it is her."

"Look," the voice said, "The guys I hired are very reliable. They told me what they did in more detail than you would want to know, but basically, they got into her hotel room and cleaned out all her stuff. They caught her and beat her to death, then they threw her naked body in the river. They took her stuff and her car to a rather expensive chop shop.

Her things were burned, they removed all the VIN numbers from the car, and they cut it up for parts. All the evidence is gone."

The phone was dead for a moment before Margret continued, "Was the body ever found?"

"I don't know. The whole thing happened way out of town. I don't follow news from out there, and I don't want to know. Actually, we wanted the body to be found. If a pretty little girl just disappears it starts a manhunt. Those are the type things that make national news. Remember Jonbenet? But if they find the body it goes down as a carjacking and the case is closed."

"Just the same," Margret said. "Something isn't right. It seems impossible, but I know what I saw."

"Do you think this patient knows our arrangement?"

"He didn't seem to," Margret said. "If he did why would he come as a patient, and especially one with such a crazy story? I think he has dissociative identity disorder."

"Has what?" said the voice.

"Multiple personalities. It could be that he has two personalities. One that spends time with the girl and one that doesn't. The one that doesn't either pulls dream images from the other or remembers the other's experiences in his dreams."

The voice didn't believe it. He said, "I have a different theory. He could be a Fed."

"A what?"

"FBI, IRS, CPD, it doesn't matter which letters you choose. They may have a hint and they are fishing for more information."

Margret was getting angry, "You told me we could do it without anyone knowing. That we could transfer the money without leaving a trail. That we could move it, launder it, and take possession of it without anyone knowing."

"We can and we are," the voice said trying to sound reassuring. "Everything is in place. Nothing was missed. All the assets will be liquidated, and the money moved within a week."

"A week?" Margret had a hint of panic in her voice. "Do we have a week?"

"Look, if you think it is too dangerous, maybe you should leave the country for a while. Didn't you say you wanted to buy a place in Caernarfon Wales?" he said.

"Oh no," Margret replied. "That wasn't the plan. I was supposed to have enough money to do whatever I want whenever I want for the rest of my life, not go into hiding. Besides, I'm not going to leave you alone until the deal is done. We have too much on each other for either of us to let the other out of our sight."

"We have to find out what this patient of yours knows," said the voice. "Make another appointment with him. Try to get him talking. Maybe we can learn who or what is behind this."

Margret reluctantly agreed and the call ended.

* * *

Dan had left the doctor's office and he stood on the street waiting for a bus to take him north to his train station. It was a busy, noisy street, but to him it felt peaceful after that session. Just as he was feeling the peace of the noisy street his cell phone rang. It was Dr. Keller's office asking to set up another appointment. Dan didn't really want another appointment, but he reluctantly agreed. Even so he made an excuse and put it off until Thursday. At least that would give him three days to recover.

He got home early enough to have dinner with his mother. He felt bad that he hadn't told her everything that was going on, but he still couldn't. He couldn't explain it to himself, much less to his mother.

After dinner he watched some TV and went to bed. What seemed like moments later he was on a mountain trail. There were white granite, mountain views and dense vegetation all around. The view could only be described as majestic. The trail was so inviting that Dan wanted to start hiking. He figured that Abbi never seemed to have any trouble finding him, so he started to walk.

He hiked up the trail. It was a stone path on the side of a mountain. To his right was a drop off into a deep valley. The valley was lush and green. Beyond the valley were towering mountains. On his right, a mountain climbed above him. He walked a long distance; it felt like it could have been an hour or more. It was quiet and peaceful.

He turned a corner and there sitting on a log was Abbi waiting for him.

"Did you have a nice hike?" she said.

"It is beautiful. I've seen pictures of places like this, but I've never been to them. Is this an actual place? Where is it?" Dan replied.

"It is a real place. I think it is someplace in Peru. We used it for a last dream.

"It was for a young man. He had always wanted to hike this trail, but it never worked out. We helped him hike it in his last dream. The trail goes on for miles." Abbi motioned down the trail. "At the end there are some ancient ruins. The man got there and stood at a perch above the ruins. He was enthralled just to be there. While he was gazing at the scene the Dream Maker came and stood next to him. They stood for the longest time just taking in the scene. The

Maker seemed to appreciate the beauty as much as the hiker. After a while they both left together."

"I guess there was no dance party after that," Dan said.

"There was a huge party!" Abbi said. "While he was hiking there were Dream Players and Technicians hiding in bushes and behind rocks the whole way. Last dreams are exciting, and everyone wants to see them. After they left, the Technicians built a big bonfire in the middle of the ruins and we all danced around it for the rest of the night. We probably looked like a bunch of uncivilized natives, dancing around a big fire. It was great!"

Dan didn't know what to say after that. He stepped over and sat next to Abbi on the log.

"Did you go see doctor scary?" Abbi asked.

"Ya," Dan said. "One thing for sure. You were right. They don't know anything about dreams."

"What did she say?" Abbi asked.

"She does think you're real, but not in the way you think. She thinks that I know you in the waking world. That somehow, I saw you and somehow forgot. Maybe I was infatuated with you so much that you keep coming up in my dreams."

"Did you see me someplace?" Abbi said playfully. Her cagey smile came back to her face.

"No, well, I don't think so," Dan replied, "It might be, but if you made that much of an impression, I would think I would remember."

"Actually," Abbi paused. She looked embarrassed. "I'm the one who saw you."

"What?" Dan said.

"I wasn't going to tell you, but I might as well now. A while ago I was in one of your dreams. I was a bit Player sitting at a conference table. You were dreaming that you were in a meeting with your coworkers at your company's office in Scotland. You were talking to your friend and describing your home in America. But then, you told your friend 'actually I am there right now and I'm dreaming that I'm here.' I was amazed. No one in dreams knows they are dreaming. I got curious about you, so I volunteered to be in more of your dreams.

"I enjoyed being in your dreams. I know it's silly, but I did. I wanted to do something nice for you, so I asked the Dream Master if I could write a dream just for you. He said I could, so I wrote the dreams you had on the train with the pretty girls. Boy did I mess that up. Writing dreams is harder than I thought. I felt so bad. I had to explain. I had to apologize. That's why I brought you into the Dream world and, well, you know the rest."

Dan didn't know what to say. He was as confused as ever. Abbi's story made sense in an odd sort of way. He even thought he remembered his Scotland dream, well maybe. He woke up in his bed. It was 3:00 AM. He sat up and swung his legs over, so that he was sitting on the side of the bed. He reviewed the dream in his head. Of course, his imaginary friend would be attracted to him. What, was he going to do, dream up a woman who hated him? He felt tired, laid back down, and fell asleep.

The Dream Maker

Chapter 6
Discoveries

Work the next day was busy. It was full of the usual meetings, phone calls and telecons. Dan did his best to stay engaged, but thoughts of the conversation from the night before kept drifting into his head. He had seen the Cognitive Psychologist twice and still had questions about his own sanity. He was nagged by the feeling that it might be better to be insane and know Abbi then to be sane and not know her. He pulled her drawing out of his brief case and stared at it. She seemed real. But at the same time everything around her was not.

At that moment John, one of his coworkers, came in with some papers.

"Hey Dan, are these yours? I found them on the printer."

"Yea, I forgot I printed them. Hand them here," Dan said.

John came around Dan's desk to hand him the papers and saw the drawing.

"Where did you get the picture? It looks great," John said.

"I bought it from an artist in Logan Square," Dan said, while he was thinking that he didn't even have to lie about that.

"Interesting," John said. "That model was in here a few weeks ago."

Dan looked at John with disbelief. "No. She wasn't. That's not possible."

"I'm tell'n you. She was here. I saw her. I talked to her," John said.

"You have to be mistaking her for someone else," Dan said. "This is someone that the artist made up in his head. He didn't have a model."

"Dan, there is something about me that you probably don't know. I'm a savant when it comes to remembering faces. I can't remember my wife's birthday or what I had for breakfast, but faces stay in my brain. I'm telling you. That lady was here. I think your artist was lying to you."

Dan had an urgency in his voice. "So you talked to her? What did you talk about? Who is she? Why was she here?"

"It was really awkward," John said.

"How's that?" Dan asked.

"She was asking about Karl," John said

"Karl?" Dan said. "What did you tell her?"

"I didn't. I couldn't. I didn't want to be the guy who told her that the guy she was coming to see had committed suicide," John said.

"So, she didn't find out?" Dan asked.

"She did, well, I think she did," John said. "I brought her up to Human Resources. I figure that they pretty much give out bad news for a living."

"Who did you take her to?" Dan said.

"Tia. She is the only human in Human Resources."

"Thanks John," Dan said. He was trying and failing to sound nonchalant. "I'm curious. I'll see if I can catch Tia later." Later was as soon as John left.

Dan entered Tia's office. It was a small room with a built-in desk. Tia had it decorated with travel posters of destinations from all over the world. Dan knew Tia because they had worked together on staffing for several of his projects.

"Hi Dan. Can I help you?" She asked.

"John in IT said that he brought this girl to see you a few weeks ago." Dan used the picture on his phone instead of the larger drawing.

"Yes he did," she said. "That was uncomfortable. He really set me up. She was looking for Karl."

Dan let go with questions. "Why did she want to see Karl? Was her name Abbi? What did you tell her?"

"Whoa, slow down. One question at a time. The name Abbi doesn't sound right. Do you know her?" she said.

"I met her a while ago, but I can't say I know her well. Are you sure about the name?" Dan said.

"I'm not sure, but I think I wrote it down. Let's see if I can remember where I put it," Tia continued to talk while she shuffled through her desk drawer. "She is from St. Louis.

She was adopted, but her adoptive parents are gone. She thought she was alone in the world, that is, as far as having relatives, until she did one of those DNA tests. The test showed that she was related to Karl. Karl thought that he didn't have any relatives either, so after exchanging a bunch of emails she was supposed to come here for them to meet. She tried to go to his house, but for some reason she couldn't get there. So, she got a hotel someplace.

"Oh, here it is. Her name is Elizabeth Hastings. That's her cell phone number."

"Elizabeth Hastings?" Dan was puzzled. Everything in his world puzzled him right now.

"That's the name she gave. We talked for a long time. She wanted to know more about Karl. I probably told her more than I should have. She was difficult to say no to," She said.

"I have no doubt about that," Dan replied under his breath.

Dan copied the name and number before he left. When he got back to his desk he tried to call, but an automated voice told him that the phone was not available.

He left work as early as he could. When he got off the train in Elgin he didn't drive home. Instead, he drove toward Bartlett, and Karl's house. He had checked a company directory before he left work, so he had the address. He thought maybe Abbi or Elizabeth, or whatever she is called might be there, or at least there may be a clue someplace. On the other hand, he thought all he would actually be able to do is drive by an empty house. But still, he had to try.

Dan used the GPS on his phone which brought him right up to the gate of a gated community. He chided himself for not thinking that the CEO of a major company would live in a secured place. He was picturing a nice neighborhood, but not a group of mansions. Still, he had gone this far, so he pulled up to the gate.

Dan rolled down his window and the guard said, "Can I help you?"

"I'm looking for someone. I was told she may be staying at the home of Mr. Karl Schmidt." Dan gave him the address.

"Mr. Schmidt doesn't live here anymore. His house has been sold and it is sitting empty," the guard said.

"OK. Well maybe you've seen my friend." Dan pulled out his cell phone. "Her name is Abbi or Elizabeth Hastings."

"Why yes. She was here. It was right after Mr. Schmidt..." He didn't want to say more.

"It was sad about Mr. Schmidt," Dan said to let the guard know that he knew what happened. "I'm looking for the girl. Can you tell me anything that might help me find her?

The guard thought for a second. "She left her name and phone number. I'm not sure why, but I pinned it to the board here." He pulled it off and handed it to Dan.

The paper had the same name and number that Dan already had, but to be nice he took it anyway and drove away.

Dan felt down. He knew that going to Karl's house was useless, but he had a spark of hope that maybe there would be some piece of the puzzle. He laughed at the thought. Piece of the puzzle, he didn't have any of the pieces, just a sketch of a girl that some people think they've seen.

He went home and had dinner with his mother. In the middle of the meal her phone rang, and she left to talk to Dan's aunt. He sat alone thinking about how he was at a dead end. All he had was a name and a disconnected phone number. He pulled the piece of paper out of his pocket and thought that maybe he could have the handwriting analyzed. No that's ridiculous. How about if he had Abbi write the same thing so he could see if it matches. No. If he imagined her, he would just imagine the same signature too.

He stared at the paper. It was neat handwriting like he would expect from a girl. He dropped it on the table and took a bite of food, then almost spit it out. He managed to swallow, as he picked up the paper again. The paper was on the little note pads they give you at hotels. Tia said she went and got a hotel when she couldn't go to Karl's. It was from an Extended Stay Hotel near the interstate. That's 10 minutes from here.

Dan finished his dinner as quickly as he could. He made up an excuse about having to run out to store and asked his mother if she needed anything as cover. Then headed for the Extended Stay.

He walked into the office of the hotel. It was a small area with a counter. There was a deserted area in back of him where they served breakfast.

A lady came out of the back room and positioned herself behind the counter. "Do you have a reservation?"

"No. Actually, I'm here looking for a friend and I wonder if she is staying here. Her name is Elizabeth Hastings. Sometimes she goes by Abbi," Dan said

"She's your friend?" she said.

"Yes."

"You don't seem to know what happened," she said.

"No. What?" Dan could see her hesitating. It reminded him of John not wanting to talk about Karl.

"It's OK. Whatever it is. I need to know," he said

"She was kidnapped. At least most of us here think she was. It was about four weeks ago. She checked in for one night. Someone said she made a trip into the city and when she came back, she booked the room for another week. I think about five days into that one of our regulars saw her get kidnapped. Joan lives here year-round. Every day she sits on the bench by the picnic table. That day she saw two men carry suitcases to the girl's car. Then they went back in and carried the girl out. She was beat-up bad. Her arms flopped around like she was dead. She might have been dead."

Dan had that feeling of constrained breathing you get when you first hear that a friend passed away. "You called the police, right?"

"We sure did," she said. "They filed a missing persons report, but I don't expect they are going to do anything about it."

"Why?" Dan asked.

"I talked to the officer. They don't believe she was kidnapped. I forgot to tell you that Joan was drunk at the time. Actually, she's drunk all the time. She gets lonely in her room and starts drinking. Then she comes out there to let it settle, I guess you could say. Anyways, the police didn't think she was a credible witness. Plus, they said that kidnappers don't take the luggage with them, and they use their own car. They think she didn't want to pay the bill, so she just left. I tried to tell them that she paid by credit card, but they didn't pay any attention to me. There's a report on the books, but that's about it."

"Well thank you," Dan said as he turned to leave.

"Wait," she said, "You said you were her friend?"

Several thoughts flashed through Dan's head about how to answer, but left it with, "Yes. We are close friends."

"Wait here. I've got something for you," she said.

The lady disappeared into the back room and came back moments later with a notebook.

"Take this," she said. "She came in here one night and asked me to put this in the hotel safe. I explained to her that each room has its own safe and there is no hotel safe. She said she didn't want to keep it in the room, and she insisted that I keep it hidden here. She was hard to say no to. The police looked at it and didn't think it had anything to do with the case. You take it. Otherwise, I'm just going to throw it away."

Dan took it. It was a spiral bound notebook with many pages of handwriting. Some pages had papers taped in like a scrapbook. He thanked the lady and left for home. It wasn't a long drive home, but all the way the story haunted him. What happened to the poor girl? Is she connected to Abbi? Is there anything he can do? In the movies kidnappers always take their victims to warehouses. There are lots of warehouses around here. Maybe he should scour all the warehouses in the area. No. That's stupid.

All those thoughts were swirling in his brain when one hit him hard. What if those men killed her? What if he wasn't dealing with a dream person at all? What if Abbi was a ghost? A chill came over him. For the first time since this whole craziness started, he was truly afraid. He had gone to a psychologist, but now he was thinking that he should have gone to a priest.

That evening he dreaded the idea of going to sleep. He spent a lot of time doing searches on ghosts and how to deal with them. Generally everything he read was useless, but it did seem that it isn't a good idea to tell an oblivious ghost that they're dead. They can get very angry and turn into a monster. It was hard to imagine Abbi turning into a monster. It was hard to imagine her not happy.

As hard as Dan tried to stay awake, he fell asleep in the recliner in the den. Moments later he found himself back in the busy Dream Maker tunnel. The hall was bustling with Players and Technicians moving to their next assignment.

Abbi was there and greeted him, "You're later than usual."

"I had some things I needed to look up on the web. I don't think I finished, but I must have fallen asleep because here I am," Dan said.

"Well, we need to get going. We have an assignment. It is a dream that the Dream Maker wrote, so we need to get there, and we need to do it right," Abbi said.

They started walking down the hall. Dan needed to say something, but he was afraid to be too blunt. It took him a moment to come up with something.

"How many dreams have you been in?" he asked.

Abbi was caught off guard. Her mouth opened to answer, but nothing came out. The answer should be in her brain, but it wasn't. It was like when you forgot to put your keys in your pocket. They should be there, but they aren't, but why and where are they?

Abbi hesitated, and stumbled, "A... A lot."

She saw an opportunity to change the subject. "Come this way," she said. "There is something I want to show you."

She guided Dan down a dark hallway. It was lined with doors. Each door had a round window.

"This is a fun place," Abbi said. "This is where children have their dreams."

Dan looked in one of the windows. There was a small boy on the floor of a play-room playing with a toy dinosaur.

"It looks like he's having fun," Dan said.

"We don't have time to watch, but if you could stay you could see the toy dinosaur turn into a real one and chase the boy around the room," Abbi said. "Boys like dinosaurs, but there isn't much adventure to playing with plastic ones on the floor. However if a plastic one becomes a real one, well, that's adventure."

Dan looked in the next window. There was a child clutching her bed. The bed was raised above the floor and under it was a monster. Dan thought to himself, 'when she wakes up she'll be running to crawl into bed with her mother.'

Dan moved on to the next window. There was a girl in her bed looking up at the ceiling. Above her was an opening chopped open by fire axes and two firemen were there with their pet Dalmatian. Dan expected her to be afraid, but instead she was laughing and pointing at the dog.

Abbi waved at Dan to start him moving. "Sorry we can't stay longer. Children's dreams are always great. I wish I could be in them, but those dreams are done by a different group of Dream Players. Maybe someday I'll get a chance."

Dan barely heard what Abbi was saying. Seeing the children's dreams reminded him of a dream he had when he was a child. There wasn't much too it. No monsters or strange happenings. It was just an image of a very long tightrope with a man slowly sliding down it. There was no background or anything around. It was sort of like the blue bubble he found himself in the night Abbi brushed him off. The man wore tights like a circus performer as he slid down the rope with his hand outstretched as if to keep his balance. His feet didn't move they just quietly slid down the rope.

It wasn't much of a dream, but for some reason that he never understood that dream scared him. It happened over and over and every time he woke up afraid. He started to think that if he knew then what he knows now, it would be silly to be afraid. But still, he wondered.

He walked farther down the hall. It seemed to go on forever. He hoped that maybe if he could see the tightrope, or better yet talk to the Player that was in his dream long ago, he could find out what it was all about.

Abbi was getting irritated. She didn't want to be late for a dream that the Maker had written. She cleared her throat and Dan finally looked at her. He realized he was in trouble and started walking back toward Abbi.

Abbi clasped Dan's upper arm and hurriedly guided him through an invisible door, where he found himself in an airline terminal. It was a departure gate at O'Hare Airport with a flight leaving for Seattle. Dan knew where he was. He had been to that terminal or one just like it many times before.

Abbi gave him some coveralls and had him sit in the waiting area. Players were already seated and looked like they had been waiting for a while, although Dan knew how quickly they can assume a role, so they may not have been there very long.

"Just sit here and be one of the people waiting for the plane to start boarding," Abbi said.

There were other Players there. Some were sitting with him. Some standing and milling around. Soon the dreamer appeared. He put down his bag and walked close enough to the information screen to see how long it would be to departure. Satisfied that the airplane was on-time he tried to pick up his bag. But it was stuck to the floor. He pulled and pulled until the bag stretched like rubber. Then suddenly it let go and flew into the air taking the dreamer with it.

He got up. The Players were starting to form a line to board the airplane. Dan stood up and followed their lead.

"The food is awful on this flight," one of the Players said to the dreamer.

Another Player whispered to him, "The seats have spikes. It hurts to sit in them.

Two more Players stood in back of him. The first one said, "Why can't we get on the plane?"

The second one answered, "Because the pilot isn't here. We can't fly without a pilot. Oh, wait, there he is."

The dreamer looked over and saw the pilot. He was a thin elderly man with a heavy grey mustache. He was wearing thick coke-bottle glasses. As he walked toward the gantry door the dreamer could see that he had a book open and was reading as he walked. As he passed the title was visible, 'How to Fly an Airplane.' As soon as the pilot passed, a shadowy Player came up and whispered in his ear and the dreamer disappeared.

Dan got back with Abbi. "What was that all about?"

"I don't know completely, but I think that The Maker wanted to give that man a message," Abbi said.

"How will he be able to remember it?" Dan asked. "The Eraser whispered in his ear."

"They are called erasers because that is what they do the most. But they can do the opposite too. They can make a dreamer remember. Then we could call them Cementers," Abbi laughed.

"Couldn't he have plainly stated his message?" Dan asked.

"The world is a complicated place. People have to decide what they believe and what they don't believe. That dreamer has all the information he needs. It is up to him to decide if it came from a powerful Dream Maker, or if he imagined it," Abbi said.

Dan thought about how he was trying to make the same decisions. He woke up in the recliner in the den. He couldn't see a clock, but he knew it was well after midnight. He dragged himself out of the chair and into his own bed for whatever was left of the night.

* * *

The next day Dan was back on the Metra train heading to work. He was pulling out his laptop to do some work when he noticed Elizabeth's notebook. He had forgotten that he had put it in his briefcase. Instead of the computer he took out the notebook. It was a simple 5 by 7 inch spiral bound notebook. There was no writing on the cover, but there were some papers hanging out of it.

Dan started to thumb through the notebook. He noticed the same neat, flowing handwriting that was on the paper with her name and number. The first pages were list of names. It looked like genealogy. 'Probably Elizabeth was planning to compare notes with Karl to determine how they were related,' Dan thought. 'No wonder the police weren't interested.' He did notice that there were several Abigails on the list. Was that just a coincidence?

Ten or fifteen pages in were lists with expenses from her trip. Gas, food, a few other things. Dan thought that it must have been a budget trip and she needed to keep track of every penny. 'I wonder if she knew she was traveling to see the CEO of a major Chicago corporation.'

After that the notes seemed to be less organized. Some were just names or titles. Some were notes to herself in sentence form almost like a diary. At first Dan didn't think much of it. It seemed like meaningless chatter, but as he continued to look he started to recognize bits and pieces. There was the name "The Never-Alone Foundation". Dan remembered seeing the flyer at Dr. Keller's office. A lawyer named William Windom. Even the name Dr. Margret Keller. Various numbers and addresses. It seemed meaningless. Dan put the notebook back in his briefcase.

During slower times at work Dan went back to thinking about Abbi and the whole situation. He had never dealt with a ghost before. In the movies they seem so scary, but Abbi acts like a friend. Dr. Keller wasn't going to cure him of a ghost. Well, that is unless it was an imaginary ghost. How could it be imaginary? People in the building he was in at that moment had seen her. Others had seen her killed. He had her notebook in his briefcase.

Thinking of Dr. Keller reminded him that he was supposed to have an appointment with her the next day. He called her office and cancelled the appointment.

An hour later Dan's cell phone rang. It was Dr. Keller.

"Dan, my assistant told me that you cancelled your appointment for tomorrow. I don't think that is a good idea. If we are going to make progress, we can't quit. I know I was a little firm with you in the last session, but I will try to give you more space," she said.

Dan wanted to keep this as short as possible. "No. I don't need to come. I have information now that explains everything. I just need to use it."

"Are you sure, because…"

Dan cut her off, "No. It's over," and he hung up.

As he put his phone away, he thought, 'Wow, she must be hard up for patients.'

As soon as the call ended, Dr. Keller made another call.

"Will, this is Margret." She was calling the same person as before.

"He cancelled his appointment. What did you find out?" she asked.

"Well, he doesn't work for any law enforcement agency that I could find. That doesn't mean that one of them didn't hire him just for this. All the checking I could do says that he is who he says he is. Why did he cancel?" he said.

"I think he knows. He said that he canceled because he has the information. Right before he hung up, he said the words, 'It's over,'" she said.

"Look, Margret, I know you don't like the idea, but it looks like we are both going to have to disappear for awhile," he said.

"If he goes to the law, we will both have to disappear forever," she said. "I can get used to the idea of laying low for awhile, but I won't be a fugitive for the rest of my life. We need to solve this problem."

"I hate to give the boys another job. Every time we use them, we increase the risk that they will make a mistake and it will point back to us. The law coming after us for the money is one thing. Coming after us for this is a whole different ballgame," he said.

"I'll start making arrangement to leave, but we can't leave a mess behind. Daniel Andersen has got to go!" she said and ended the call.

In the afternoon Dan got sucked into a meeting in the large conference room. In most meetings he makes a point to sit at the table. It is more comfortable if he wants to take notes or open his computer, plus he feels like it is better for his image. But not in this meeting. Here he sat firmly in the row of chairs along the wall.

The meeting dragged on. Some man with a southern accent droned on about risk management metrics. Dan didn't even know why he was there. He started thinking about the notebook. He considered pulling it out of his briefcase right there but thought better of it. But some parts were coming back to him from the train ride this morning.

'The house closed before,' he thought, 'what did that mean?'

He remembered more. "The estate was settled in days. Stocks were sold without notice. Never Alone Foundation got it all. NAF didn't keep it. There is no NAF."

Then Dan's thoughts turned to Abbi. A ghost that didn't know she was dead. What would it take to free her? Maybe if her death were avenged, or if not avenged at least explained.

The meeting ended and Dan went back to his desk. Work was the farthest thing from his mind. He pulled out the notebook and looked through it again. There was that phrase, "The house closed before." What could that mean? Was she talking about Karl's house? He could look at that. Cook County property records were all online. He searched for Karl's address. Of course, it had recently sold. Wait, it sold twice. The first was a title transfer and the second a regular sale. Dan scribbled the dates on a post-it note. Then he did another search for Karl's obituary. The first transfer was before he died. He went back to the property site to see where the property was transferred. The first was to the Never Alone Foundation, the second to someone named Glenn Olson. Did Karl donate his house?

Dan went back to the notebook. The pages were full of accusations written in short phrases, almost as if they were in code. But none of the accusations were backed up with documents. The notebook would be worthless in court. But he had the evidence on the house and the notebook was right.

Dan hesitated. He knew what needed to be done, but he also knew the risks. Police would go to a judge and get a warrant, then they would get a computer expert to search databases to see if the accusations were valid. Dan couldn't do that, and he didn't think he could get the police to do it either. But he had more skill in that area than any police computer expert. If they found out they would call it hacking. He could be fired, or worse, he could be prosecuted. But his thoughts turned to Abbi or Elizabeth and what they did to her and he decided he had no choice.

He started his quest, but not before taking every precaution he knew. He set up an account for a fake employee. He routed his searches through multiple servers. He was careful never to stay logged on to any one site any longer than he had to. He made sure to only read data and when possible, clean up any leftover records.

He researched the Never Alone Foundation. He looked in their bank account. It was with a bank he had never heard of and it was empty. But there were transactions. Lots of transactions and millions of dollars. For each transaction the money came in and immediately went out. It was obvious that it was being used for money laundering. This was the starting point and from there the money spread out in all directions. Dan followed some of them. It was a sophisticated system; whoever set this up was no amateur.

Dan continued to look. He didn't want the records on his computer, so he printed the data. It was already late, and no one was around. The money came in from various places, but in discrete bursts of time. As if it came from one scam at a time. Dan could research some of the names where the money came from. He didn't recognize the names of the account holders except one, Mr. Karl Schmidt.

Then Dan started to look the other way to see where the money went. It was difficult. It went from account to account and even became cryptocurrency at one point. He didn't have enough time to trace all the paths, so he picked a few and followed them through. They ended in two places, the account of Dr. Margret Keller and someone named William Windom.

Dan didn't completely know what was going on, but he could see that these two were running some kind of an operation. It was starting to make sense. Karl was the perfect victim. He was rich and had no heirs. Get him to sign some papers and no one will question his estate. That is until someone named Elizabeth shows up.

It was a nice theory, but Dan still had doubts. Karl was a top businessman. His base salary was millions of dollars a year, and everyone in the office wondered what he got in stocks and special benefits. He wasn't stupid and he wasn't naive. How could he fall for it? Dan couldn't understand, but evidently, he did.

It was getting late, and Dan had to get going if he was going to catch the last train. He had an inch high pile of printed papers on his desk that could land him in jail. He went to the supply cabinet and got a large brown envelope.

He stuffed the papers in the envelope and took it to the server room. At least it had a cypher lock, and it wasn't his office. Among the racks of computer there was an opening where a backup power supply had been removed for repair. Dan put the envelope in the opening and screwed the cover in place. No one should be going in there and if he was unlucky and someone found them, they wouldn't know who put them there.

Dan got to Union Station later than he wanted. As he hurried through the terminal a television caught his eye. It was a cable news station. He paused to watch the video of a damaged airplane as the announcer said, "One person was killed, and two injured when an airplane slid off the runway at Seattle's Sea-Tac Airport."

He thought about the dreamer and wondered. 'Did he still take the flight? Was he one of the victims? Or was he home thinking that it could have been him on the news.' There was no way to know.

Chapter 7
Flying High

Dan caught the last train and walked in his front door well after midnight. His mother didn't wait up. He was exhausted and fell asleep on the bed fully dressed. Moments later he was back in the Dream Player service tunnel.

Before he could get his bearings, Abbi was talking to him. "I'm glad you're here. I was wondering if you were OK," she said.

135

"I had to work really late," he said. "It's not like I can call you and let you know."

"It's OK. I hope you got it all done. Anyway, you missed my assignment. I don't have any more tonight, so I was wondering if you would want to do something fun?" she said.

"Do you ever do anything that you don't think is fun?" he asked.

"Everyone has their moments," she said. "The important thing is to uncover the fun in whatever you are doing. Although fun might not be the best word. In every situation you get a choice. You can look for the good and enjoy what you can, or you can see the bad and, well, have a bad time. You can choose for yourself, but whenever I can, I choose to find joy."

"I wish I were better at that. Maybe I can learn it someday," he said.

"It gets easier the more you do it. Now. Do you want to do something fun, or not?" she said.

For a moment the things he was learning in the waking world came to mind, but then he told himself to put those thoughts away and said to Abbi, "Let's go!"

Abbi guided him down the tunnel. It was bustling with Players and Technicians scrambling to their next

136

assignment. As they walked by one of the halls Dan heard a strange crying, growling sound.

"What was that?" he asked.

"That's where they do the animal dreams," Abbi said.

"Animal dreams?"

"Sure. Animals dream too. It is a whole different group of Players for animals. I don't know any of them," she said.

"That is true," Dan said. "I used to have a German Shepherd and I remember watching him dream. I always wondered what an animal could possibly be dreaming. Do they go for a walk and suddenly remember that they forgot to put on their fur?"

Abbi laughed. "I really don't know what they dream, but we can look in the windows and see."

They turned the corner and walked down the hall. It was lined with doors and like the child dream hall each door had a window. Dan looked in the first window. There was a gray cat crouched and ready to pounce on an unsuspecting mouse.

Dan looked over at Abbi and said, "Looks like a normal cat."

"Look again," Abbi said.

Dan looked through the window. The mouse had grown to twice the size of the cat and was now chasing it around the room. Dan wondered if the mouse was actually an Animal Dream Player.

The next room had a dog. Dan thought it looked like a beagle. At one end of the room was a human sitting in a chair. The human had a tennis ball. He threw the ball and the dog retrieved it. Every time the dog brought the ball to the human, the human gave him a thick juicy steak. It was a very good dream.

They moved on. Dan looked in a window and there was a raccoon. The room looked like a park and there was an unattended picnic basket. The raccoon quietly snuck up on the picnic thinking he was going to get a nice easy meal. But he couldn't get the basket open. He tried and tried, but he couldn't get to all the wonderful food inside.

"We have to go," Abbi said. "I've got a Technician waiting for us."

Dan followed her back to the main hall.

"Do you know what the most common dream is?" Abbi asked.

"I'm thinking it is falling like we saw in that room a while ago," Dan said.

"You're close. It's flying. Do you want to go flying?" she said.

Abbi guided him around a corner and through a door. He found himself on the roof of a tall building in the middle of a city. Dan looked at the buildings. It wasn't Chicago. It might be New York, or it could be a generic city that the Technicians just made up.

"The Techs have everything ready. Flying is easy. Watch me. First you start running. Take big steps. Make every step bigger and bigger. Then stop touching the floor and you're flying," she said.

Abbi took a few steps back, and then she started running. Right before she got to the edge of the building, she was airborne. She flew away about a block, made a loop and came back. As she made a slow pass over Dan she yelled, "You try."

As Dan was taking steps back, he was thinking, 'She just told me how to take off, but not how to land.'

Just like Abbi said, he started running, taking as long of strides as he could. As he ran, he felt the resistance of the roof below him disappear, and like Abbi, he was flying. They flew together sometime high, sometimes making low dives close to the street below. They streaked around tall buildings and played superhero tag. A few times he lost Abbi, but it didn't worry him. She always seemed to be able to find him.

Dan saw a passenger liner flying overhead and pointed. Together they took off to try to catch it. They came up behind the airplane one to the left and one to the right, then they started to overtake it. They flew parallel one on each side.

Dan flew close and looked in the window. There were no passengers. Dream Players were too busy to take time to fill an airplane with passengers for another Dream Players entertainment. But he looked all the way through and saw Abbi in the window on the other side. She had her face pressed against the glass just to make a funny face.

Abbi broke away and flew above the aircraft. Dan looked up and saw her motion to him. She shouted, "Follow me!"

She took off flying straight up like a rocket. Dan followed. He looked below and saw the city getting smaller and smaller. It looked like the Earth itself was shrinking behind him. He looked up and could see stars. He and Abbi's climb slowed to a stop as if they were at the top of a giant arc, then they started to fall back to Earth.

Dan lost Abbi. He couldn't tell where she went. He started to gain speed as he descended faster and faster. He could see fire building up around his body. The ground was approaching fast, and he couldn't stop! He was going to crash!

Dan woke up, and thought, 'She couldn't resist putting a dream trick at the end.' It was 6:00 AM and time to get up for work.

$$* \quad * \quad *$$

The next day Dan went to work, but he couldn't concentrate on work. There were scenes of flying with Abbi popping into his head and when they weren't there, there was the research he had done the night before. He didn't know what to do with that information. He wondered if he took it to the police, would they do anything with it or would they arrest him? There still is a possibility that all those transactions were legitimate.

He had written a list of the people who transferred money to the Never Alone Foundation on a note pad on his phone. He figured that having a list of names on his private phone wouldn't be incriminating evidence. He pulled out his phone and scanned through the names. He knew what happened to Karl, but he wondered about the others. Actually, he didn't completely know what happened to Karl. It could be that he was tricked into transferring everything he had and when he realized that he had nothing left decided to end it all.

He started doing searches for the other names. Who were those people? Could he talk to any of them? He found the first one, a Chicago entrepreneur. He had a very successful chain of restaurants. He died last year.

The next name was too common. Dan couldn't tell if he had found the right person or not. The next was a successful businesswoman, deceased. Followed by a wealthy, but very old man, deceased. Followed by another common name. Dan could confirm that half his list was no longer alive and half he couldn't tell. It didn't seem like a coincidence.

He wondered if they had a last dream. If they did what would the last dream of a multimillionaire be like? He thought of the woman at the Aragon Ballroom. All she wanted was to be able to relive that one moment of her life. And there was that young man. He just wanted to hike that mountain trail.

He thought, 'What was that woman's name?' After some thinking, 'Oh yeah, Dorothy. I wonder if I could find her obituary. To be in her twenties in 1944 she would have to be in her late nineties now. Maybe over one hundred.'

He searched and found seventy eight Dorothys that had died in the area in the last month. Of those, nine could have been her, but none for sure.

Dan started to think about Dorothy' last dream. How grand it was. How special. How loving the Dream Maker was with her to gently take her with him. Then he had another thought. Why didn't Abbi get a last dream? If she had had one, she surely would have talked about it. She died just a few weeks ago, so it would have just happened. Besides, the Dream Maker takes the dreamer with him and Abbi was still there. The Dream Maker knows she's there. He talks to her and gives her assignments. She speaks so highly of him all the time.

'I wonder why…' A revelation came over him. He said out loud slowly and deliberately, "Because she's not dead. She is dreaming too. But she's constantly dreaming."

Dan thought about what kind of person could be constantly dreaming. There was only one answer.

Dan made up an excuse and left work immediately. He couldn't wait even a minute. As soon as he got to his car, he drove to Saint Joseph Hospital. It was the nearest hospital to the train station, and not too far from the hotel where Elizabeth was abducted. He hurried in the front door not sure what to ask or who to talk to.

He went up to the front desk, "I'd like to talk to whoever is in charge of security."

"Have you experienced a problem?" The lady behind the desk asked.

"No. Well, nothing to do with the hospital. Who can I talk to?" Dan said.

"Our head of security is Wayne Saylor. Let me see if he is available." She picked up the phone and a minute later gave Dan directions to his office.

Dan went to the security office. Wayne's office was a small square room. He had a wooden desk and two guest chairs.

"What can I do for you?" he asked.

"My name is Dan Andersen. I'm looking for someone. I have a friend; her name is Elizabeth Hastings. I was told that she was in a violent carjacking. A witness said that she was thrown in the back of a car unconscious and driven off. I think she may be in a coma somewhere. They might not know her name."

Wayne picked up a piece of paper and looked through the pages. "We don't have any Jane Does here at the moment. I get a daily briefing. I would know."

Dan hung his head and turned to leave.

"Hold on," Wayne said, "Let me make a few calls. I need a little more information, a description, age, weight, etc."

Dan gave a description of Abbi. He had never seen Elizabeth, but he hoped they were the same. Wayne made some calls while Dan listened.

"Sherman Hospital, four miles north from here has a Jane Doe that might fit the description. The security man's name is George Grossman. Go to the front desk and ask for him, he will be expecting you," Wayne said.

Dan hurried to Sherman Hospital. The front desk ushered him back to George Grossman's office. It was similar to Wayne's office, but the walls were decorated with plaques and awards. Dan glanced at a couple of them. They were all from law enforcement.

"You're the young man Wayne called about?" he said.

"Yes. I'm looking for someone," Dan said.

"I see. We have a person who matches the description you gave to Wayne," he said. "How do you know this person? Are you a relative?"

"No. I'm a friend. Actually, more of an acquaintance." Dan was struggling with what to say. "I haven't known her long. I don't even have a picture of her. I had this drawing made."

Dan showed the picture of the drawing on his phone.

"Bob Weber."

"What?" Dan asked

"You've been to see Bob Weber. This is a retirement job for me. Most of my career was in law enforcement. Every police department in Northern Illinois knows Bob and he knows them. He is kind of a legend among police investigators. I know a Bob Weber sketch when I see one. I see you went for the up-sell," George said.

"Huh?"

"Bob always tries to make a little more money by making a photorealistic drawing. Usually police don't go for it, but it's good that you did. Anyway, any friend of Bob's is a friend of mine. Let's go to ICU," George said.

George led Dan to the Intensive Care Unit and introduced him to the head nurse. The nurse brought Dan into the care area. Dan took one look and was stunned. It was her. She was unconscious in bed with tubes in her nose and mouth. Dan turned his head and stepped away. He didn't think of himself as an emotional person but seeing her like that caused him to well up. He had to leave the room to regain his composure.

"Are you OK?" the nurse asked gently.

"Yes. Sorry. It was such a shock to see her like that," Dan said.

"Are you a relative?" she asked.

"No. Just a friend. It's complicated," Dan answered.

"It is good that you could identify her. We were hoping a relative would come. We need someone with the ability to make the decision about continuing care," she said.

"Continuing?"

The nurse took a deep breath. "You should know that her condition is very serious. She is only being kept alive by the machines. If the machines are disconnected, she won't live. Hospital management has petitioned a judge to make the decision, but that takes time and, well, isn't as personal as if it is done by family. It is something a relative should decide."

"Tell me about how she got here. What do you know about how she was hurt?" Dan asked.

"We don't know how she was injured. She was found by some canoers on the Fox River," she said.

Dan remembered what Abbi said when she heard Dr. Keller's name. 'I was thrown into the ocean.'

"She was naked, so there was no identification on her. They found her floating and at first thought she was dead. Fortunately, one of the canoers is an EMT. She started CPR right away and kept her alive until the Paramedics arrived. She was so bad they had to airlift her here," she said.

Dan remembered Abbi's words, 'Then I was picked up by a bird. A noisy bird.'

"We put her on the machines right away. It is the only thing that kept her alive," she said.

Dan thought, 'Then I was attacked by snakes. Snakes in my mouth and nose and arms.'

"Can I spend some time with her alone?" Dan asked. "I'd like to talk to her."

"Certainly," she said. She moved a chair close to the bed, then left and closed the door behind her.

Dan pulled up a chair and sat down. 'It's her,' he thought, even though in many ways it didn't look like her. Her face was bruised, and her hair was stringy. She had the look of someone that had lost weight in an unhealthy way. She had IVs in her arms and an oxygen tube in her nose. In her mouth was the tube from a ventilator.

"Hi," Dan said as softly as he could, "This is Dan. Do you know me or am I just in your dreams? I can't believe you are real. When I first saw you I assumed you were something out of my imagination. But you were so real. As I got to know you, it was hard for me to believe I could imagine someone like you. I had never met anyone like you, so although I believed you were real, I had to keep telling myself that you were not. I honestly thought I was going insane.

"Then came the double shock of learning that you were a real person and learning what happened to you. I honestly thought you had died and that I was seeing your spirit. I must admit I was afraid, but not of you. You were the most alive person I had ever met, even when I thought you were dead. So, I've gone from thinking you were imaginary, to thinking you were a spirit, to," Dan took a breath, "to this."

Dan sat silently for minutes. He didn't have any thoughts. He just stared at the damaged person before him.

He took a deep breath and continued, "I hate seeing you like this. It really hurts. You were the one who told me to find the good in everything, well; I'm having trouble seeing it here. The nurse says you don't have a lot of life left. If you were awake, I would probably have trouble telling you that, but if you can hear me, you probably already know.

"But I guess there is some good. If you weren't here, I never would have been in your dreams, and I would never have met you. But..." Dan paused again to regain his composure.

"You know I do need to thank you. I am starting to see that I am a different person than I was two weeks ago. Two weeks ago, I thought my life was pretty good. But now I see that it was empty. I worked; in fact I did very good work. But I'm seeing that each project I did took some of me and didn't give anything back.

"Two weeks ago, all that was in my life was work with little breaks to eat and sleep. There were no relationships. There was no future. Nothing to look forward to, the work I did was not worthwhile, no one special to love. Then, suddenly you pulled me into a whole different world.

"It's hard to explain and I'm still not sure what it means, but it showed me that I can't live the life I had been living. I have to start looking for a new path in life.

"It would be nice if you could walk down that path with me, but..." he paused, then continued. "If you leave, I won't be able to go into a dream world anymore, but my waking world will never be the same. I will find a new path."

Again he stopped to look at her. It was Abbi. But not the Abbi he knew. She was full of life. This Abbi was running out of life.

"You know, I would have had a very different reaction two weeks ago if the nurse told me that they were looking for someone to make a decision about 'continuing your care.' I don't want you to go. I don't want to live my life without you, but you showed me what a last dream looks like. The Dream Maker doesn't consider death to be a bad thing at all. The Dream Players throw a party. I hope I can come to your last dream."

Dan felt like he ran out of words. He sat looking at her until a nurse came in to check on her.

He went home and had dinner with his mother. He still felt like it was futile to try to tell her about the events of the last two weeks, but he did tell her that he had a friend in a coma in the hospital and that she wasn't expected to live. When she asked where he met her, he just said that he met her on the train.

That evening Dan did not look forward to going to bed. What was he going to tell Abbi? How could he even be around her knowing what he knew now? But he couldn't go without sleep and eventually he had to lie down.

Moments later he was on the Metra train gliding through the Chicago suburbs. He looked out the window, but he couldn't tell where he was. A second after that the scene shifted and he was on a different train. Now it was an old steam train that was rattling and clicking along. He could hear the airy steam whistle and the sound of the giant pistons as they chugged in turn propelling the train forward.

There was no one else on the train. Dan looked out the window. There was scenery going by, but it just looked like a desert out west, so he couldn't tell where he was. He looked ahead and saw a conductor coming down the aisle. He realized that for the first time in two weeks he was in his own dream instead of someone else's.

"Tickets please," the conductor said.

"I don't have a ticket," Dan replied.

"No, you don't. You're riding for free," the conductor said. "You are our guest, and we always treat our guests well. You look like you have had a tough day."

"It was a very hard day," Dan said.

"Because you learned about Elizabeth," he said.

"You know about that?" Dan said.

151

"Yes, and that is why I need to talk to you alone. I gave Abbi a very involved assignment tonight. She will be busy all night. I expect that the next time you see her she will be apologizing, but don't worry about it. It was my plan. Just tell her it is OK.

"Something you need to know, is that Abbi doesn't know anything about Elizabeth. As far as she knows she is a Dream Player like the rest of us and has always been a Dream Player. I know it will be hard for you, but you must not tell Abbi about Elizabeth. The best advice I can give you is to think of them as two different people. You have a friend who is in the hospital and another friend who is healthy. You can enjoy being with the healthy friend even though you are worried about your sick friend.

"Abbi is very special. We don't know why the Dream Maker decided to let her into our world. We think that maybe he saw her in a coma, trapped in her own body and decided to let her be free in the dream world. It had never happened before. In fact, at first, many of the Dream Players resented it. It was like allowing an amateur to play on a professional team. But any Player that had an assignment with Abbi quickly fell in love with her. Her zest for life was contagious and all the Players where happier after those assignments. I had Players volunteering to be assigned with her," the conductor said.

"Why are their names different?" Dan asked.

"The Erasers felt that if she kept her name, it could trigger memories of her waking life. It could bring back the pain, just like when you said Dr. Keller's name. When she first came, she picked her name before the Erasers suppressed the memories of her waking life. We don't know why she picked the name Abbi," he said.

"Her grandmother and grandmother's aunt were named Abigail," Dan said matter-of-factly.

For a moment the conductor looked a little irritated that he didn't know that.

Dan continued, "So, Elizabeth isn't doing well. If she dies will Abbi be able to continue as a Dream Player?"

The conductor sighed, "No. When Elizabeth's time in the waking world is over the Dream Maker will write a last dream for her. At the end of the dream, he will take her away. Normally we look forward to last dreams. It makes us happy to see someone from the waking world go with the Dream Maker. There is nothing better for them and we feel like we have finished our work. But there won't be any dancing when it is Abbi."

"I can understand that," Dan said, "It is amazing, or maybe it's not, that Abbi is the only one."

"She was the first one, but not the only one," the conductor said.

"There's more?" Dan asked.

"One more," the conductor paused, "You." He paused again. "I told you that we didn't understand why the Dream Maker allowed Abbi in. We understand you being let in even less. You don't have any infirmities. You don't have any special dream talents, if you pardon me saying so. He didn't even have an Eraser suppress your memories. In a way you are a bigger enigma than Abbi. But the Maker wants you here, and here you are. I am not the one to question it, so you are welcome."

The train whistle blew, and Dan woke up in bed. It was only 11:00 PM. He got a drink of water and went back to bed. He had trouble sleeping the rest of the night.

Chapter 8
Warning

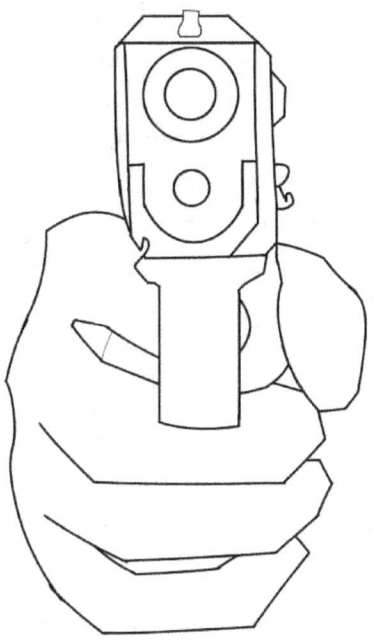

The next day Dan went to work. He was still wondering how he was going to be able to be around Abbi now that he knew the truth. It was easy to say that they are two different people, but they aren't. People who are in a dream are the same as people who are awake. They are afraid of the same things. They react the same way. There is no difference. But Dan resolved that he would do his best to make them two different people. It is what the Dream Master asked him to do, and it was the right thing to do.

The day dragged on. Dan felt like he was going through the motions. His mind was filled with the events of the night before, and even more the shock of seeing Elizabeth for the first time. He made sure to leave work early enough that he could stop by the hospital and see Elizabeth. He saw how closely their worlds were tied together and he wanted to be able to monitor her in the waking world as well as spend time with her in her dream world.

He caught the 4:10 train and headed back to Elgin. It was early and the train car was nearly empty. The stress of the last twenty four hours was catching up with him and he nodded off.

The next thing he knew he was sitting at his desk at work. He was at his desk, but nothing looked like his office. It could have been any office, but somehow, he knew it was his.

John came in and said, "Hey Dan, happy Mother's Day."

Dan looked at him, "It's not Moth…"

John cut him off, "I'm taking my mother out for dinner tonight and you better do the same. Mothers are important and you wouldn't want to ignore yours on Mother's Day."

Andrea, who actually worked at their New York office came in and said, "I hear you're taking your mother out for dinner. You better leave at eight o'clock. That's when the food is the best. If you leave early, it won't be cooked. If you leave late, it will be burned. Studies show that eight o'clock is the very best time."

Tia from HR came in. "You only have one mother. You better take her out tonight if you love her, and you need to take her car. She won't like it if you take your car."

Dan remembered being on the train. He guessed that he was dreaming. He thought Abbi promised not to bother him on the train, but here he was. Three people telling him that it was Mother's Day and that he had to take his mother out tonight at eight o'clock.

Dan looked up and was surprised. He saw his mother standing there. That was odd because she had never been to his office before. He wasn't sure she could find it if she had to. She was dressed in a house dress that looked like it was out of the 1950's. She pointed her finger at Dan and insisted that they go out and that they go out that night at eight o'clock.

Dan just replied, "Yes, ma'am."

As his mother was walking away Dan heard a soft giggle. He was pretty sure it was Abbi playing the part of his mother. He woke up and after clearing his head a little, called his mother. She told him that she would love to go out, and that it was the strangest coincidence, because the night before she had dreamt about going out to dinner with him.

Dan stopped at the hospital before going home. The nurse told him that Elizabeth was the same and that they were working with a lawyer to get a judge to rule on ending treatment. Dan thought about what the Player had told him last night. He knew that if he lost Elizabeth he would lose Abbi too, but he was at a loss about what to do.

He had the thought that he could get a lawyer and get custody of her. That way he could keep her alive as long as possible and he could be with Abbi. But as he sat looking at her condition, he had to hold back tears. Even though she wasn't conscious, she had to be in tremendous pain. What kind of a monster would he be to leave her in pain, just so he could be with her in dreams? It wouldn't be right, but he still hoped that there would be something that would make this right.

He stayed as long as he could. When he was alone with her, he told her about Abbi and the wonderful place where she was. The fun she was having and how carefree she was when she was there. The Dream Master told him not to tell Abbi about Elizabeth, but he didn't see how it could hurt to tell Elizabeth about Abbi.

He looked at the time. He had to go get his mother. He thought how the Players were right. Going out with his mother for dinner would be good for him. It could help him get his mind off of, well, everything.

He got home with enough time to change before they went out. They left right at eight o'clock and went to a small diner not far from their house. He was glad the Players pushed him to do this. The food was good, and it was the best conversation he had had with his mother in a long time. Dan was enjoying himself enough that he tuned out the rest of the world, even though the street outside was noisy and there were constant sirens as emergency vehicles drove by.

Dinner ended and they headed back to their house. They turned on their street only to find that it was blocked by a police car. Dan found a place to park, and they started walking. Two blocks down they saw a house burning. It was their house!

They went up to the first fire fighter they saw and Dan said, "That's my house!"

The fireman had a serious look on his face. "Was there anyone inside?"

"No. It is just my mother and me and we were out."

"Thank god," the fireman said. "The blaze is so hot that we haven't been able to get near it. If there was anyone inside, we wouldn't have been able to help them. Come with me. I'll take you to the fire chief."

The fireman walked down the street with Dan and his mother. As they got closer to the command car Dan could see the house better. It was fully engulfed in flames. He could see fire coming out the windows and a large hole in the roof. The firemen were spraying huge amounts of water on the building, but it didn't look like it was doing anything at all. The fireman introduced Dan and his mother to the chief and left to go back to work.

"You lived here?" the chief said.

"Yes, the two of us," Dan said.

"Did you keep explosives or large quantities of flammable liquids in the house?" the chief asked.

"No. Well, maybe a can of gas for the lawnmower."

"No. That wouldn't do it. This is a big fire, but it looks like an explosion to me. It might have been a gas leak. Were you having any trouble with gas appliances? Did you smell anything?" the chief asked.

"No."

"We will do a full investigation and we'll get to the bottom of it, but it will be a day or two before it is cool enough for us to look through the debris. You need to just stay away and don't try to salvage anything until we're done. We'll be in touch. In the meantime I'll make a call to the Salvation Army. They'll find you a place tonight. They'll also get you some clothes and toiletries. Was that your only car?" he said.

Dan looked closer to the house. His car was destroyed. Almost as if it had its own fire.

"We have another car," he said.

Dan and his mother watched for another hour while their house burned and collapsed into a pile of soot. The man from the Salvation Army arrived and was very sympathetic. He set them up in a suite type hotel and got them the basics to keep going. They probably could have taken the car and found a place, but they were in such a state of shock that it was hard to think.

It was 2:00 AM when Dan finally laid down to sleep. He soon found himself back on the dock on the quiet lake. He was sitting on the bench and Abbi was already sitting next to him.

"I am so sorry about last night," she said, "I got this assignment that took a really long time. I was in the dream of a lady with Alzheimer's. In the waking world her memory is failing, but in the dream world she can talk and tell stories like she used to do. In the waking world she can hardly walk, but in the dream world we went for a long walk down a country road. We talked for hours. For a little while she was free and not trapped in her own body. She was so happy to have someone to talk to that I just couldn't leave her."

"It is amazing that the Dream Maker would be so kind as to allow someone to be free in their dream world when they are really trapped in their own body in the waking world," Dan said, knowing that his words had two meanings.

"I loved talking to her, but I really am sorry I abandoned you," Abbi said.

"It's alright," Dan said.

Abbi has been lost in her apology, but she finally realized that Dan was not the same as usual.

"You don't sound all right, "Abbi said. "In fact, you don't look good at all. What's wrong?"

"My house. It burned down. It exploded and there is nothing left," he said.

"That's terrible! I am so sorry. It must be why you're so late. How did it happen?" she asked.

"I don't know. The fireman said it would take a couple days before it will be cool enough for them to investigate," he said. "Everything I owned was in that house. In fact, I would have been in the house too if you hadn't given me that dream warning."

"Is that what the dream was for? It didn't make any sense to me. The Dream Maker wrote it, but I thought he wanted you to pay more attention to your mother," she said. "In fact, it came at the last minute. We didn't even have time to make your office. We just used one from a different dream."

"Well, he saved my life," he said.

"So what happens next?" she said.

"I guess tomorrow I start over. There is a lot to do. I don't even know where to start," he said.

Abbi and Dan talked into the night. After the trauma of the house, it felt good to have someone to talk to. Dan thought about how it felt safe to talk to her. It was partly because she was understanding and easy to talk to. But it was also because he knew he was talking to the dream persona of a person in a coma, so anything he said wouldn't be repeated, or at least he didn't think that it would.

He woke up not sure where he was. It took a minute to remember that he was in a hotel room. He fumbled for his phone. It was eight o'clock on Saturday morning.

Dan got up and wandered into the main room. The suite had one main area and two bedrooms. His mother was already up and dressed. She had the television on showing the morning news.

The TV chattered, "No one was hurt yesterday when a house in suburban Elgin exploded and burned to the ground. At the height of the incident more than 60 firefighters were involved in fighting the fire which may have been caused by a gas leak. For more on this story, we go to…" Dan muted the television.

"We're famous," Dan said under his breath, as he looked around for a pad of paper and a pen to start making lists of things to do.

* * *

At the same time at her home in the city, Dr. Margret Keller was furious! Her hands shook as she picked up the phone to call her business partner.

"You moron, you absolute idiot, you, you… I can't believe you let this happen. What were you thinking? You were supposed to fix the problem and look where we are now. How could you let those goons use a bomb? This is all over the news. It is all over the country. And what's worse, he's still alive! The reports all say that there were no injuries. No injuries!"

"Now Margret, calm down," Will said.

"Calm down? I won't calm down. We were just fine, but you wanted to do one more job. One more that was bigger than all the rest put together, you said. It was a sure thing, you said. This guy's the perfect candidate, you said. Then the girl shows up and starts snooping around. I don't know how she found as much as she did, but your scheme wasn't as airtight as you said it was.

"Then you said you could solve the snoop problem, but you botched that too. Then that lunatic boy starts seeing her in his dreams. He still could be a spy. We don't know. You said you would take care of him, but look at the news," she fumed.

"Margret, I had him tailed since you told me about him. If he were a cop, he wouldn't have been so oblivious that he was being followed. I don't think he knows anything. If he was going to go to the law, he would have done it already. If he were going to try to horn in on our action, he would have done that. Besides, by following him we found the snoop," he said.

"You found the girl? Where is she?" she said.

"We don't need to worry about her. She's a vegetable in a hospital out near where they dumped her. She's just costing the hospital money and they want to pull the plug. I have a colleague who's taking it to a judge and I can assure you, they will turn off the machines very soon. That is what the hospital is paying him to do. That problem will take care of itself," he said.

"I knew he was seeing her someplace, but why the crazy dream story?" she asked.

"Like you said, he must be some kind of a loon," Will said.

"Look. Loon or not he is a problem. A problem that needs to be solved," she said.

"It will be a few days. After the last job, the boys left town for a while. They want it to cool down a little before they come back," he said.

"I don't like it. I'm leaving the country tonight and I don't like leaving loose ends behind. And, by the way, I won't let you be a loose end either. I have my money secured, and I have enough on you to put you away for the rest of your life or worse. After this, you live your life and I'll live mine. If they come after you, leave me out of it and I'll do the same for you," she said.

"Where are you going?" he asked.

"Don't you worry about it. I can contact you electronically and you don't need to know where the messages come from. Now take care of that loose end and we can both rest better," she said, and she ended the call.

* * *

Dan spent the day starting to build his life again. He called his boss to tell him that the company laptop was now a piece of charcoal, and that he would be off for a few days. He talked to the insurance company for both the house and the car. He bought some clothes and rented a car. He thought about how you take for granted all the things in your life until they are gone. About how the smallest thing can mess up your life when they are suddenly missing. At that moment, the smallest thing was his phone charger.

By afternoon he was exhausted and just sat in a not very comfortable chair in the hotel room watching TV. His phone dinged with a text message. He pulled it out of his pocket expecting it to be a message from his mother.

Text: "Dan I need your help."

There was no name on the screen, just a number.

Dan's phone: "Who are you?"

Text: "I am a Dream Player. I came into the waking world to save Elizabeth, but it's harder than I thought, and I need your help."

Dan's phone: "What can I do?"

Text: "I can't function in the waking world like I thought I could, but together we can save her. Come get me and together we can save Elizabeth!"

Dan hesitated. 'Was this real?' Then he thought about how the only ones who have ever been let into the dream world were him and Elizabeth. No one else would even know what a Dream Player is. No one could possibly know about Elizabeth. It has to be real.

Dan's phone: "Where are you?"

Text: "I'm at the train station, on the West side of the tracks at the far South end of the parking lot. Please come quickly. Help me."

Dan's phone: "I'm coming."

Dan grabbed the keys to his newly rented car and headed to the train station. As he drove, he wondered what the Dream Player would look like. In the dream world they could look like anyone they wanted, but is that the same here? They must be able to come here. They know what everything looks like. They keep up with current trends and incorporate them into people's dreams.

It was Saturday and the parking lot at the train station was nearly empty. Dan drove to the south end of the lot. There was only one car parked there. It was an expensive looking BMW. He parked and got out of the car. The door of the BMW opened, and a figure got out.

Dan was surprised. "Dr. Keller, what are you doing here?"

"I'm checking up on you, Dan. Are you OK?" she asked in a sarcastic voice.

Dan's heart started beating faster. He realized that something was wrong. But the situation was still confusing him.

"I'm... I'm fine. How did you..." he said slowly.

"How did I get you to come here? I recorded your sessions. I took notes. You told me all about your fantasies of Dream Players and the girl. Of course, you'd come if you thought one was in trouble," she said.

"What do you want?" he asked.

"I have everything I want, and I intend to keep it. I'm not going to let a little psycho like you take it away," she said.

She reached into her purse and pulled out a gun. It was a small gun. Dan could barely see it in her hand, but he couldn't mistake the round end of the muzzle pointing in his direction. Instinctively he froze and raised his hands in front of him.

Dan spoke as deliberately as he could, "I don't want to take anything away from you."

"I don't care what you want. I'm leaving the country tonight and I don't want anyone coming after me. You are the last loose end," she said.

"Wait!" Dan said.

Suddenly all Dan saw was blackness. The sounds of the city stopped. There was no pain. All he could sense was darkness and silence. He thought, 'She must have shot me. I wonder if I am still standing. No, couldn't be. I must have hit the pavement by now. Did I fall forward or back? I must be lying there dying.'

Instantly, Dan found himself in the Dream Player's service tunnel. It was the usual scurry of Players and Technicians moving back and forth going to their assignments. He felt his chest in several places to see if there was a wound. There wasn't. He thought, 'I'm not dead. But I may not have a lot of time.' Then he thought, 'Where's Abbi?'

He stopped a Player and asked where Abbi was, but the Player didn't know. He stopped another and another. None of them knew. He changed his question and asked where was the closest Dream Master. The Player pointed to another Player that was busy giving instructions to a small group.

Dan burst in, "Can you find Abbi for me? I need to see her right now!"

The Dream Master looked a little annoyed, but he had his group wait while he attended to Dan. He told Dan to wait where he was. He disappeared through an invisible door and moments later came back with Abbi.

"What are you doing here?" Abbi looked very confused. Every time Dan had come in the past, she had arranged for him to come. He shouldn't be able to come on his own.

"I've been hurt. I was shot. I don't know how bad. I'm not dead. At least I don't think I am, but I could be dying. I don't have much time," he said.

Abbi didn't know what to say. "How? Who?"

"Your Dr. Scary, Dr. Keller, shot me," he said.

"Why would she do that?" Abbi asked.

"You were right when you said something isn't right with her. She has been part of a plot that has been killing people for years and she has stolen a lot of money. I have to stop her," Dan said.

"How can you stop her? From what you just said you are dying and if you are here you must be asleep or at least unconscious," she said.

"I have to write a dream and I need your help," he said. "I have to do it now!"

"You can't write a dream. Only Dream Masters can do that," she said.

"I know what dream I need to write, I need for you to get me the Technicians, Whisperers, and Erasers," he said.

Abbi didn't know what to do. She saw the Dream Master that had brought her. He was back with his group giving them instructions for their next dream. She waved for him to come over. When he came, she explained what Dan wanted.

The Dream Master said, "You can't write a dream. It would be highly irregular. It isn't possible."

Dan put his hand on the Master's back and guided him away from Abbi while he talked to him. Abbi couldn't hear what they said, but moments later the Dream Master told Dan to wait there. He disappeared through an invisible door and quickly returned. He announced in a loud voice that the Dream Maker wants us to produce Dan's dream and that they should spare no effort.

Dan took the Dream Master aside and started talking to him. Abbi stayed back. She couldn't hear what they were saying, but the conversation looked very animated, with both talking with their hands and pointing in various directions. Abbi was trying to tell if they were arguing or collaborating. Every so often the Dream Master would call over a couple of the Players from his group, give them an assignment and send them off on some mission.

Finally, after what seemed like a very long time the Dream Master gathered his group of Players again and gave them a briefing on what their new mission was going to be. He explained that this dream was more important than what they were going to do, so some people were going to have less interesting dreams tonight because they had other duties.

The Dream Master who was so hesitant to work with Dan had changed his mind. He gave his group their final instructions and encouraged them to do their best for the Maker. He finished his briefing by looking at his Players and shouting, "Let's do it!"

Chapter 9
Revelation

In the Chicago neighborhood of Logan Square, Bob Weber, the artist that drew the picture of Abbi, was finishing up a portrait of a married couple who had commissioned the painting for their anniversary. He had a large photo of the couple on an easel as he transferred the image onto his canvas.

He had finished the easy part and was bogged down in the details. It made him tired, so he took a minute to sit in the overstuffed chair he used for live models. He quickly fell asleep.

Suddenly he woke up. Dan was standing in front of him.

"Who are you? How did you get in here?" he asked.

"Do you remember me?" Dan said. "I'm Dan Anderson. You did a portrait of the girl in my dreams a week ago."

"Oh yes, you're the kid with the good memory," he said. "What are you doing here? I hope you don't want your money back."

"Not at all. I am in trouble, and I need your help. I've been shot and I need for you to catch my killer," Dan said.

"You don't look like you've been shot," he said.

"I was shot by a woman named Dr. Margret Keller in the parking lot of the train station in Elgin. Evidently, I am still alive, but I may be badly wounded. I might be dying," Dan said.

"You don't know how badly you're hurt?" he said.

"No, everything went black as soon as she pulled the trigger," Dan said.

"But you're here talking to me. I don't think so. How do I know anything you say is true?" he asked.

"Do you remember the drawing you did for me? How would you like to meet the girl that was in my dreams?" Dan said.

Abbi had been standing directly in back of Dan so she couldn't be seen. She stepped to the side where Bob could see her. Bob looked at her like an art student seeing a master painting for the first time. Abbi couldn't help grinning like she had just jumped out of the shadows at a surprise party.

"It is her," he said. "How…"

"Don't worry about how. She is real. You can see her, and you have to believe me," Dan said.

"Well, you do have one solid piece of evidence. So, you want me to catch your assailant?" he asked.

"There's more," Dan said. "A lot more." He grabbed Bob's hand and led him toward the door. Before they got to the door the scene shifted and they were at Dan's office outside the server room. Dan told him where they were, including the company name and address.

"This is the company server room. The combination to the door is 2095. Let's go in," Dan said.

They entered the room. The Dream Master had kept Abbi away, so it was only Bob and Dan.

"There is a much bigger plot going on. Dr. Margret Keller and a lawyer named William Windom are working together to steal money and murder the money's owner. Keller would screen her patients looking for people who were rich but had no family attachments. Every few months to a year she would come across a candidate. She would get them to will their fortune to an organization called The Never-Alone Foundation, or they would forge papers to make it look like they did.

"After Windom had the papers done, they would arrange for the person to commit suicide. Keller is a Cognitive Psychologist. People come to her because they are having trouble, but she could make her records look like they were very troubled, so no one questioned their death.

"I have a list of victims. There may be more. Their last victim was Karl Schmidt, the CEO of this company. It was Mr. Schmidt's death that started to undo their scheme. They didn't know that Mr. Schmidt had just found a relative through a DNA ancestry company. At the time of his supposed suicide, he was supposed to meet with this relative, whose name is Elizabeth Hastings.

"Elizabeth was supposed to only come for a weekend but when she found that Mr. Schmidt had died she extended her trip and started to investigate. She has a way about her. It is hard to tell her no. She was able to amass a lot of facts. But she made the mistake of not realizing that Dr. Keller was a part of the plot. She talked to Keller, and Keller realized that she was too close to the truth.

"Keller and probably Windom arranged to have her killed. They hired two men to kill her and make it look like a carjacking. They beat her and threw her body into the Fox River, but she survived. She is in Sherman Hospital in a coma right now.

"I don't know how, but somehow, she started appearing in my dreams. The drawing you made opened the door for me to find Elizabeth and do some of my own investigation. I got too close, and Keller lured me to the parking lot at the train station in Elgin and tried to kill me. Tonight, she is planning to leave the country. She has to be stopped."

Bob looked at Dan and said, "That's all fine and good. Do you have any evidence?"

"You are in the server room at my company. You will need a screwdriver to remove this panel," Dan said.

He took a screwdriver out of his pocket, removed the cover and pulled out the stack of papers.

"Here you will find printouts of many of the financial transactions they made. It proves they stole the money. I'm sure police investigators can prove the murders. I didn't know what to do with it because I had to hack computers to get the data. I was afraid I would be in trouble, but now I've been shot and I have more important things to worry about. Keller and Windom have to be stopped. Keller can't be allowed to leave the country," Dan said.

At that moment, an Eraser came up and touched Bobs head to ensure that he would remember every word of the dream. They disappeared and Dan was left standing alone in the server room.

Bob Weber woke up in the overstuffed chair. He had never experienced a dream like that. It was so real, and he remembered all of it. In fact, he couldn't forget it. He asked himself if it could be real, but then remembered how much detail Dan remembered when he came for the drawing. Was it real? There was an easy way to find out. He reached over, picked up the phone, and called a friend at the Elgin Police Department.

"Marc, this is Bob Weber. Did you have a shooting at the train station? You did? Hum, how's the victim doing?" Pause. "I see. Can you give me a description of the victim?" Pause. "I have been given an anonymous tip. I think I can solve that case for you. But there is a lot more. I'll need for you to have the CPD get a search warrant for a company downtown. According to my source there is a whole murder theft ring. This will be a very big investigation. Oddest thing, I thought I was getting old and couldn't remember stuff, but I remember all of this."

* * *

Dan opened the door to the server room and walked out into an area of nothingness. It startled him. He had forgotten that the room he left was just a dream set. He looked around. There was no one there. He had been left behind. If he was able to do that six-dimensional moving thing nobody showed him how. He stood wondering what to do when a Dream Player appeared through an invisible door.

"Sorry," he said. "I was supposed to bring you with, but I forgot."

He took Dan's hand and guided him through an invisible door, dropped him off, and left. Dan found himself alone in a rustic wooden room with a steep staircase in front of him. There was nothing to do but climb the stairs. As he did, he felt the room moving. He was on a ship.

At the top of the stairs, he found himself on the deck of a wooden sailing ship. It had three large masts with sails unfurled. The ship was underway. The crew was busy at work keeping the ship sailing. Dan could hear the creaking sound of the wood as it moved with the waves and splashing sound as the ship cut through the water.

He walked toward the bow on the starboard side. The water was a deep blue, with only the slightest waves. Looking ahead he could see they were coming near an island. He saw Abbi. Her hands were on the rail and the wind was blowing through her hair as she watched the water go by. She was wearing a long white dress. Dan thought that was odd. Unless she was in costume for a dream, she had always dressed in the same clothes, but today she looked like a first-class passenger on an ancient sailing ship.

She saw Dan. "Isn't it wonderful? We're explorers. The first ones to see these islands. What a great adventure!"

Dan didn't say anything. He joined her watching the water and feeling the fresh air.

The ship came close to the island and started sailing all the way around it. They could see palm trees, mountains and waterfalls on the land. It was a tropical paradise. They spent hours together. Abbi was captivated by the whole experience.

Dan looked at the detail of the ship, the water, and the land. He started to realize that this was not normal for most dreams. Then it struck him. This was Elizabeth's last dream. He stayed with Abbi trying not to show how upset he was.

The ship sailed into a cove and dropped anchor. Dan watched as a smaller boat made its way from the shore toward their ship. It had a crew onboard rowing and another crewman in the stern steering. There was a lone person in the bow, standing as the boat came closer. Dan guessed it was the Dream Maker.

The Dream Maker came aboard and joined Abbi and Dan. Dan stood as close to Abbi as he could. Abbi realized that this was her dream. She was confused. Dream Players don't have last dreams. They don't dream at all.

"Don't be afraid," he said. "Abbi, it is time for me to tell you that you are not a Dream Player. In the waking world your name is Elizabeth Hastings. Six weeks ago, you were violently attacked. You were hurt so bad that you fell into a coma and have been ever since. When you were first injured, a Dream Master staged a dream for you. I saw you in that dream and saw that you couldn't be confined the way you were. You had to be free.

"I wouldn't let you be trapped in your waking world body, waiting for the end. I brought you here, into the Dream World where you could live and enjoy the time you have left. To spare you the pain of the waking world I had an Eraser help you forget Elizabeth. You became Abbi. I loved your spirit from the beginning. Now all the Dream Players love you."

"How did I get here?" Dan was thinking and was surprised that the words came out of his mouth.

"Let's just say that Abbi is a difficult person to say no to," the Dream Maker said. Then looking at Abbi, "But Elizabeth Hastings' time has run out and it is time for you to come with me."

Dan felt adrenalin pouring through his dreaming veins. He could feel his heart beating, and his chest tighten. He cried out, "No! You can't take her!"

The Dream Maker didn't say anything. He just looked at Dan.

Dan tried unsuccessfully to stay calm. "The waking world needs her. There isn't another like her."

"But it is her time," the Dream Maker said.

"Then take me instead," Dan said.

Abbi looked at him with a shocked expression.

"You will survive your injuries. You have a long life ahead of you," the Dream Maker said.

"It would be a life without Abbi. No. Take me instead," Dan said.

Abbi was speechless. She wanted to say something, but when she opened her mouth, nothing came out.

"But it is her time," the Dream Maker said again.

"Then take us both," Dan said. "I won't go back alone!"

The Dream Maker stared past both of them, as if he were in deep thought. The smile he had on his face when he arrived had turned to a look of contemplation.

After a while he turned to Abbi, "Abbi, you can decide. I will grant Dan's wish in that you can both come with me or both return to the waking world. But before you decide you should know that it won't be easy for either of you in the Waking World. You are both badly injured. If you go back, you go back to your damaged bodies. There will be a long and painful recovery."

Dan took a step back, away from Abbi.

Abbi stood alone. She looked at Dan. It wasn't just Dan. He represented her life in the waking world that was cut short. If she chose to go back, she couldn't be sure she would be with Dan, but she would resume her life. She would see her friends again. She would take back what was taken from her, and even if it was in a damaged body, she would win against the evil that put her here.

Then she looked at the Dream Maker. He had been so good to her. In fact, it was only now that she had learned how good he had been. He didn't have to let her into the dream world. He could have just left her in her dying body. She has seen many last dreams. They were always happy. The Players always threw a party. She didn't know where The Maker takes those people, but the Players would know if it weren't a wonderful place.

She looked back at Dan. She was deciding his life as well. She could trust the Dream Maker to take care of him if they went with him, but just like she was cheated out of her life Dan would be cheated out of his.

Abbi was torn. She wanted to go with the Maker, and she wanted to go back. She took a deep breath, took Dan's hand, and said, "Let's live."

* * *

Suddenly, Dan could only see black. He heard a clicking sound and a sound like mechanical breathing. He heard people talking but he couldn't understand what they were saying. He tried to move his arm, but pain shot through his body. He opened his eyes. His sight was blurry. He could make out the image of his mother and someone else standing near. Others that he didn't recognize were running around, but he couldn't tell what they were doing. His vision became clearer. There were machines with numbers and lines that showed his heartbeat. He was in a hospital room.

He gasped, "Where's Abbi, uh, Elizabeth? Is she alright?"

"She is going to be alright," a voice said. Dan squinted to see who was talking. It was Bob Weber. What was he doing here?

"I need to see her," Dan said.

"You're staying right where you are for now," a nurse said as she checked his vital signs.

"We'll get you there as soon as we can," Bob said. "Strangest thing, you and her came out of the coma at almost the same time. You first and then her, maybe an hour later."

"She probably had to say goodbye," Dan said in a weak voice. He knew that no one would understand what he meant.

Bob continued, "We caught your assailant and her partner. The DA has opened a Grand Jury inquiry into the whole thing. They will be out of circulation for a very long time. Now, young man, at some point you need to explain to me exactly how I cracked this case. I had to tell a string of white lies to get the information to the right place."

Dan ignored him as if he was still too groggy to hear.

He was nowhere near healed enough to be moved, but the next day he managed to talk the nurse into putting him in a wheelchair. He didn't know what to expect. Would Elizabeth even know who he is? He resolved that if he had to start over with her, he would do it.

The nurse wheeled him to the other end of the floor. She parked him outside Elizabeth's room and had him wait while she checked to make sure she could accept guests. Dan could hear her talk. He couldn't make out the words, but it was great to hear Abbi's voice. Even though it was weak it was still punctuated by an occasional laugh.

A minute later the nurse returned and pushed Dan to the foot of the bed.

Elizabeth looked up and stared at Dan. A look of disbelief and confusion came over her face. She exclaimed, "You're real?" then without thinking. "You look terrible!"

Dan tried to smile, but the movement caused a lot of pain and his smile was more of a grimace. "You don't look so hot yourself," he said. "You looked a lot better in that long white dress on the exploration ship."

The expression on Elizabeth's face became more serious. "You remember that? You were really there?" she said.

"I remember all of it," Dan said. "I remember everything we did together."

"Then, it wasn't all a dream?" she said.

"It was a dream. It must have been because I woke up after each one. But were we in some other world where dreams are put on like stage plays? I honestly don't know," he said. "Maybe it's true that dreams aren't what we always thought they were."

Elizabeth was silent for a moment, then she said, "What do we do now?"

"We do what you told The Maker we were going to do. We live," Dan said emphatically.

Elizabeth thought for a second and then said, "I don't think I know what that means anymore. I thought I did once, but not now."

"I feel the same way," Dan said. "A few weeks ago I wouldn't have even thought of the question. But I'm not worried in the least."

"Why is that?" Elizabeth asked.

"Because I know someone who knows the answer," Dan said. "She can show us the way and give us all the help we need."

"Who is that?" she asked.

"Her name is Abbi."

The Dream Maker